UNDERSTANDIN
THA
STRUGGLES
2
SURVIVE

DESTINY TYNETTA HENRY

Order this book online at www.trafford.com
or email orders@trafford.com

Most Trafford titles are also available at major online book retailers.

Printed in the United States of America.

ISBN: 978-1-4669-2142-9 (sc)
ISBN: 978-1-4669-2143-6 (hc)
ISBN: 978-1-4669-2141-2 (e)

Library of Congress Control Number: 2012905080

Trafford rev. 03/20/2012

 www.trafford.com

North America & international
toll-free: 1 888 232 4444 (USA & Canada)
phone: 250 383 6864 ♦ fax: 812 355 4082

DEDICATIONS

THANKS TO GOD FOR GIVING ME THE ABILITY TO DO THIS

JOHN AND PERSELL HENRY: FOR ALWAYS BEING MY PARENTS AND ALWAYS TAKING MY STUFF FOR THE LAST 20 YRS. I LOVE YOU AND THANK YOU FOR ALWAYS BEING HERE FOR ME.

RICHARD BROWN: TO MY DAD FOR EVERYTHING THAT YOU HAVE DONE FOR ME. THANK YOU FOR GIVING ME GOOD ADVICE AND COMING INTO MY LIFE AND LOVING ME UNCONDITIONALLY. I LOVE YOU DAD AND THANK YOU FOR EVERYTHING.

SUMMER, ARLETHIA, GAVONDA, SHAVONDA, JOHN, DIAMOND, THERESA, RICHARD, DARIUS, DUSTAN, MERCADES, CARLOS, TERRANCE, AND SUPREME. FOR BEING MY BROTHERS AND SISTERS. I LOVE YA.

MY GRANDPARENTS. MY COUSINS, MY NIECES AND NEPHEWS, MY GOD MOTHERS AND MY WHOLE ENTIRE FAMILIES. I LOVE YA ALL. AND I LOVE YA ALL. AND MRS. ANNIE FRAISER FOR BEING A WONDERFUL OTHER MOTHER TO ME.

AND LINDA AND RAHEEM JONES FOR COMING INTO MY LIFE AND HELPING ME WITH ADVICE AND WISDOM

TO HY HUBBY. I LOVE YOU

CHAPTER 1

Understanding what life is like is hard. I know because I have been through this time after time after time again. All the heart breaks and lies, I never thought that being with a man for a long time would be so hard. All the fussing and fighting plus the women saying this and that about our relationship are getting on my damn nerves. Hi my name is Tiffany Johnson. I am 21 years old and I am 5'8 and I am light skinned with long blonde and black hair. After I gave birth to my babies I had went from 110 lbs to 140 lbs. But I am still fine as hell. I have been dating my boyfriend for the past 9 years. I have already had 2 of his kids: a 2 year old little girl name Nia and a 6 month old little boy name Antonio Jr. I have been trying to understand Antonio to this day, however I am done trying. My life has been hell since the day that I was born. I have been trying to put the pieces together in my head and it still has not happened yet. I have been through men after men and I thought that I have found the right one but I guess I was wrong. I decided to rent my own apartment because things happened where I live that has caused me to move and try to make a better life for me and my kids. My baby daddy understands but I don't trust him being there without me because all those women that wanted to talk to him how I know that he is not fucking one of them. I don't want to think like that but what else do I do? I am trying but how much can I take.

ALICIA

Understanding people is the craziest thing. How can someone say that they love you and don't give a damn about you? And the things that you go through every day. 'I love you Alicia. And I will never hurt you.' I am tired of hearing this. Hi my name is Alicia Smith. I am 19 years old. I am short, I think I am 5'4 and I weigh 110 lbs. I am light skinned and I got my hair cut and dyed red before I got pregnant with my baby girl. My baby daddy said that he loved me before I gave birth to my now one month old daughter Kia and then after he started saying that she wasn't his and I slept with all his friends. And I didn't even do that. He calls me a ho, slut and it really hurts. I am better off alone then with him.

JASMINE

Understanding how a man can keep secrets from his wife is still the question that I have no answer too. I feel that my husband has been hiding something from me and I don't know what it is. Hi, I am Jasmine Smith. I am 26 years old and I am 5'6 and weigh 150 lbs with braids down my sexy chocolate back. I am just like candy. Me and my husband have been married for now 8 years now and we have 4 children together. 3 boys: 9 year old Christopher, 8 year old Kevin, 6 year old

Jamair and my baby girl Mya. Life is rough with four kids but I am working trying to make a life for us but my husband isn't doing shit to help me but I still got to get myself together to do for me and my kids. Everyone in my family doesn't want me with my husband but I can understand why. Something's happened for a reason. I am so happy that now I can think about a lot to think about. But there are a lot of things that my husband and I still have to work on and now that my one of my sister could watch the kids so me and him could go out and talk about this problems in our marriage.

TIFFANY

On some days Antonio and I get alone so well. I guess he feels bad for blacking my eyes because he decides to take me and the kids out to dinner and he is paying. I swear on some days that I love him to the point that I can't see myself with any other guy and on the others can. "Tiffany, I know that I have not told you this lately but I love you and our kids and I want you to be with me forever. Would you marry me?" Antonio asked me on one knee. It was the thing that I have always wanted but should I say yeah.

"Honey. Will you marry me?" he asked again.

"Yes I will marry you." I said jumping into his arms. But sometimes I feel that I have made the wrong decisions. I remember when I first say Antonio I was in middle school. I had just moved from Virginia and I didn't know anyone here. So he had walked up to me.

"Hi my name is Antonio. Are you lost?" He said. I was not the type that talked a lot but when I saw him I knew that he was the one. So like a month later we started to go out. I never had problems with him until I had got pregnant at 17 and lost my baby. I never forgave him for that. Now he wants to get married. What am I going to do?

ALICIA

Having a small child and trying to go to school and work is so hard. I don't get any help for my daughter at all and it hurts. "Hey can you come and watch Kia for a few hours until my mother gets off of work." I said to my baby's father.

"That's not my daughter or my problem. Don't call my damn phone again." he said hanging up. I never knew that I could fall in love with a man that is so stupid and into himself. My baby daddy already has like 10 kids by 8 females and he doesn't take care about none of his kids. When I first met him he was my everything that man would always come and get me and take me to places that I have never been. And then it changed after I got pregnant. After I got pregnant he started calling me a ho and trying to get his other baby mother to fight me and even his sister tried to fight me. But his mother knew that Kia is his baby. Sometimes a man can be so stupid and not know what the good thing it is that they have until they wake up and I am gone. How could you hurt someone and they don't even notice you after you have done all that you can to help them? I never thought that people would beat the hell out of you like he did. But I sit in the kitchen thinking about my life and it doesn't add up to me. How can I be a young women that try to do the best by people? And at the end is treated like shit. I add up all the pain from my past and it just aint making any sense. I know that I do wrong but I am not all the way wrong am I? I know that she is going to go back with him. I know that I have made mistakes before but I know that well . . . But back to the situation at hand. Things are crazy. People can treat you anyway they want to and that is so sad. Man I need to know what the hell to do now.

JASMINE

Never knowing my cousin was hard. And now that she is here I feel so much better knowing that she is here. My husband now has started to change I see that he don't talk to me about anything like he used to do in the past years before I gave birth to our 2nd child.

"Stop hitting on your brother Chris." I yelled. I have to yell at my kids all the time and my husband doesn't do anything. I clean, cook and take care of the kids and all he does is drink him 3 beers and play his stupid X box and smoking up my cigarettes. I know that my husband years ago was falsely accused of raping someone and my family knows about it and wants me to leave him but I am going to stick beside my husband no matter what anyone say about because I was there and I talked to both sides and no one said what had really happen and I believe him. My auntie had came to get my cousin today and I know what it is that she is going to tell her because this whole family needs to mind their damn business because he never did anything like that. But I am not going to get into that right now. I NEVER THOUGHT THAT LIFE would HAVE A FUNNY WAY OF TEARING YOU DOWN. RIGHT WHEN YOU'RE DOING GOOD SOMETHING BAD ALWAYS HAPPEN. My life started as a fairy tale that just deals with a lot of ups and downs. I know that there is more that is meant for me but what is it.

TIFFANY

I love my sisters don't get me wrong but they are sometimes too stuck up. They think that they are better than someone but in all reality they are not. My mother didn't raise us to think that one is better than the other. But you know what is so funny. I had her man before she did anyways but she says that I slept with him and all this stuff. I just don't know what to do with this man. How can you love a man so much to the point that you lose yourself. People do that all the time I bet. My boyfriend doesn't like my cousin. I don't know why but I don't want to ask why either. I don't feel like fighting and arguing with him at all right now. I am starting to feel like our family might be over because he don't get or understand what is going on in my life. My cousin has given me some advice that I listen to but I still deal with things my way. I love that she tries to help me but I still handle things my way.

ALICIA

People keep coming to me telling me that my baby daddy don't claim my daughter, saying that I don't know who my child's father is and I need to go find my child father and I need to stop saying that he is my daughters father. But I can't see why people is all in my damn business because they was not there when I laid down and fuck him or when I laid down and had my baby. So why are they all in my damn business? Sometimes I wonder if they want my life. My drama, my tears, my joyful baby girl. I mean my everything. As I laid my beautiful baby down in her crib. I looked at her knowing all the things it is that I have put her through. I feel so guilty like why do to I have to put my daughter through this pain. I know that she can't feel it yet and I don't want her to. I can be the mother and the father to my daughter. She don't need a damn thing from a man not even one that can't claim their own baby. Living in my own home I have things that I have to do. I had to clean up my house and put my baby to bed. As I started clean up a knock came to my door. It's my daughter's father. "What are you doing here?" I said. "Look I want to see my daughter." he said trying to walk through the door. "OH NOW YOU WANT TO SEE MY DAUGHTER AFTER YOU IS GOING AROUND TELLING PEOPLE THAT SHE IS NOT YOURS." I said upset. "Look can I please come in and we talk about it." He said still trying to come in. I decided to let him in because we really needed to talk about the situation in hand.

JASMINE

I just got done cooking dinner for my kids and as the kids ate and they was getting on my nerves.

"I want you to sit here and eat your food and behave or you won't get your dessert." I said. I tried to clean up the house so that way I can get ready to go to work in the morning but I couldn't because I still had to get the kids ready for bed, plus I get everyone clothes out for tomorrow. But I noticed that my husband has started acting a little too nice so I knew that he had got into something bad. I know that he had done something wrong. You know that you can always tell when a man does something wrong. First he didn't want anything to do with the kids or you and then he wants to take us out and spend time and money on us and its crazy because he only acts like that when he has done something wrong.

"Honey so do you want to tell me what's going on?" I said sitting on the side of the bed. He wouldn't say a word he just looked at me like I was crazy or something but trust me I am not crazy I know what the hell it is that he has done. But you know what I am going to be a good mother to my kids and I can do me at the same time.

TIFFANY

Today starts the new day for my life. I have seen that men can't understand that you can't put your hands on a woman and think that you are going to stay with them they got to be out there damn minds. I am sorry you can only hit me once and then after that no. I don't know what got into him. I mean I have kids. I don't want them to see mommy and daddy fighting. To have my 2 year old daughter look at me and cry because I am bleeding all over the floor. It's just so crazy. I never knew a man to beat on a woman. And I got his kids are you serious. I mean things were never perfect. I just don't know what to do. I mean

I love him but damn why must you beat in front of our kids and when I tell you to get out you come back begging me to let you come back because it would be different but I have heard that shit so many times that I just want this shit to be over. He and I are over. My friends tell me that I need to keep this man because he is a good man. But behind closed door you can never imagine what happens time after time again. The same thing and I am tired of it. I mean I have to small kids to raise so how I look staying in a relationship that might end my life. I got to think about my life and my kid's life.

"Baby we need to talk about the fight today" Antonio said walking into the bedroom.

"I really don't want to talk about it right now. I am trying to put my baby to sleep." I said. I really don't want to hear it. I mean it crazy.

"Look honey. I am so sorry for hitting on you." He said laying Jr. down. I don't know if it is his eyes or the way that we make love that make me fall back in love with him. I know I am fool for a little piece of dick but hell what woman don't.

ALICIA

I sit here still wondering why I am sitting here with him right now. I still can't get the answer that I need right now.

"So what is it that you want from me?" I said looking into his eyes.

"I need to know if that baby is really mine. I mean she don't look like anyone in my family." he said. How dare him. You know what I mean. I don't understand how the man that took my childhood to make me into a woman can sit here and ask me that. I mean that I know that it may have seemed like I was fast but I not.

"How dare you ask me a question like that? When we were together it was all about us me and you. I never cheated or stepped out on you even now that we are done. And you got the nerves to say that my baby doesn't look like anyone in your family and that is a lie. You aint got to lie. If you don't want to take care of her then I can do it all by myself. I don't need a man to do anything for my baby so if you're done please leave." I said walking him to the door. After he left I decided to go into my baby's room and looked at her. I wonder if I am doing the right thing for my baby. It's a question that I still can't get. But I need to know but I hope that I am.

JASMINE

My husband has been out all day today and I sit at home wondering what it is that he is doing. I missed work today because my daughter is sick and there was no one there to watch my baby girl. As soon as my husband came home I know that I had to get the answer to the questions that I need to know. I had got my kids wash up and ready for bed. I noticed that my husband has been in the room since he came into the room the while time that he has been home. I had to clean the kitchen with the food and the mess that my kids have made in the house. He never had help with the kids. I have tried to ask him to help me out but me never get a answer he just go and play that stupid x box. I am so tired of that.

"Honey where was you at all day today?" I asked walking into the room.

"You don't ask me where I been at because I can go where ever I want to." He said.

"Look, I got a reason to ask. I am your wife. That mean I can ask you any damn thing it is that I want to." I said.

"You don't have any mean to ask me anything okay." he said getting upset.

"Yes, I do you are my husband . . . ." Before I knew it he had hit me. I fell to the floor and he started punching me. I cried it felt like my world was going to end. I decided to get my kids dress and go to my mother house. I knocked on the door. I knew just what my mother was going to say but I need to come here. Whenever I need my mother she is here. And that is what I always come to my mother for.

"Who is it?" she said coming to the door.

"It is your daughter mom can please open the door." I said.

TIFFANY

I don't know what it is about him but damn. I still can't see myself being with him. But I just can't find someone that can love me with 2 small children. I had a doctor's appointment to check and see if I have any kinds of STDs but I found out that I am 3 weeks pregnant with my 3rd child. What am I going to do now that I am pregnant for the 3rd time? After I had my check up to see that the baby is doing well. I decided to go home and tell Antonio that we are having another baby. Knowing him he is not going to be too happy with this one. After I gave birth to Jr. He said that he didn't want any more kids but he said that same thing after I had Nia but my kids are my life and I will have this baby no matter what he says. I hope it's another girl. I always wanted 2 girls and a boy. Tomorrow my baby girl turns 3 years old. I have a big party planned for her.

"Nia baby girl what do you want for your birthday?" I said lying on the bed with her.

"A baby." she said. I am surprised about a lot of things that my little girl says.

"Well mommy is going to fix you something to eat and give you a bath. Okay sweetie." I said kissing my daughter on the head. I remember when I was pregnant with Nia. I was in my last year in high school and I was in class and I started getting sick throwing up in the classroom after I eat everything. I was always sent to the nurse's office where she gave me a pregnancy test and it came out positive. I was so scared because I had to tell my mother and my ex boyfriend. See at that time me and Antonio was not together but we were still having sex. But after I seen my daughter I fell in love with her it was the first time that I had seen and held a baby that small. Nia was born 3lbs.2 oz. I had her small because I went in 2 months early because Antonio pushed me down the stairs. I couldn't believe it but I had my son early to. Jr weighed 2lbs. 0 oz when he was born because I was thrown all around the house and everything. I never thought that a man would hit a pregnant woman. But he did.

ALICIA

After I told him to get out. I sat in my daughter's room for hours until she woke up. I never knew that a man can make you feel so low lower than you can ever imagine. I mean that I loved this man and now I can't stand his ass. He is just like his broke ass no good father. The only time that he wants to see my baby is when I have sex with him and I have stopped that because I am not going to give up the ass just for him to do the right thing. I mean damn what more can I do. Hell, I gave him his daughter. A beautiful little girl with a smile that would light up the world and even a room if you sit in it long enough. But was I right for kicking him out when he had something to offer? I'm still trying to figure that out as I wash and put clothes on my little girl. A woman can take only so much from a man but when it comes down to her daughter that's when she would take a lot more. I mean really a lot more. I don't give a damn about my baby daddy but I just want him to be there for his daughter. I have played the father role to long now it is his turn to be the father. I decided to call him back over. Crazy as hell as I feel but I got to do the right thing for my baby. As I put Kia into her playpen a knock came to my door.

"Come on in." I said sitting on the sofa.

"I was glad when you told me to come back over." he said walking into the house. As much as I hate to do this I have to.

"Look, I call you back over because I want you to be a part of Kia's life but I want you to stop saying that she is not yours. I mean there will never be anymore us but I do want you to be there for your daughter. I mean I can do everything I can as a mother but I can't protect her from boys like her father can. I need your help." I said as he shut the door.

"First of all I never said that she wasn't my daughter and second I want to be with you and my daughter as a family but I can't if you keep on hating Me." he said sitting by me. Damn, what do I say now?

JASMINE

My husband is still acting like he is the nicest person in the world right now. I just came back from taking my baby girl to the doctor. She was getting a little bad cold and I don't play that when it comes down to my kids. "Honey where's my boys?" I said look for a good ass reason to why my sons are not in the house right now.

"Well, your sister came by and says that she was going to take them for a few hours." he said continuing to play his game. See, I hate that shit. He doesn't never call me and tell me when someone takes my kids somewhere. When Tiffany brings my kids back she looked like something was going on in her life. And being the oldest sister I had to step in and find out what is going on.

"Sis, what's going on?" I asked as we walked into my room and closed the door.

"I am pregnant again and I don't know what I am going to do. I mean what I am going to do. Antonio doesn't want any more kids and I just don't want him to hit me anymore." She said with tears rolling down her face. I knew that my little sisters have been through a lot with just the three of us.

"Sweetie, you love this man and I can see that but you got 2 beautiful kids to live everyday for. Antonio is a great dad and man but he has some ways that needs working on. Go see mom and ask her what to do." I said like that would have made her feel better. Our mother is a woman of wisdom. With 3 girls hell you have to be but me and my sisters are my mother's life I think without us she would have a hard time in life.

DESHAWN

As a mother I always raised my 3 daughters to take care of each other and protect each other and they have always have but sometimes they try a little too hard to try to keep a bad man. My oldest daughter Jasmine is just like her father. Sweet, nice, friendly and compassionate. She will help others but that husband of her I don't agree with. He used, and abused my daughter and made her feel like shit but she is right there the way I was with her no good daddy. My 2nd oldest daughter Tiffany is out spoken like her daddy. That girl will tell you what's on her mind without thinking a 2nd about it. And my baby girl Alicia is just likes her mother. See Alicia's heart is a heart of gold because no matter what someone has done to her she tries to do better. See I raised my daughters not to look down on anyone because you never know what it is that that person has been through in their life. I raised them to respect one another because at the end of the day all you have is family. I had to find out the hard way. When my kids were little there fathers never did anything for any of them. Yes, I have 3 kids with 3 different baby fathers. But I always told myself that I will raise my girls up to never wait for a man to do something that you can do for yourself. And they all have showed me that they can't except Alicia. She is trying to do without a man but she wants the man there for his child but I love my girls no matter what path they take. Momma always got their backs.

TIFFANY

After coming from my sister's house I decided to take a walk to my mother's house being that she haven't seen the kids in a few days. My mother is a wise woman she helps me out every time that I need some help. "Good afternoon mom." I said putting the baby down on the floor and Nia ran to my mother and jumped into her arms.

"Tiffany every time I see you it seem like something is wrong so what's going on." she said. My mother is not the type of person that will hide anything that she sees.

"Well, I'm pregnant again. I feel that Antonio is going to cause me to lose the baby how he is acting. Mom I am scared like I don't want my kids to see me cry anymore and I don't have . . ." I started.

"Baby girl I have done told you. Life brings a lot of ups and downs. But you got to make a decision. Is your life better with this man or without? You got to make that decision baby. I can't make it for you but what I can tell you is that I want you to be happy no matter what your decision is." My mom said. I kissed my mom on the check and sat down and watch a little bit of television with her. That when my sister Alicia came into the room.

"Hey mommy." she said putting the baby on the bed.

"Hey baby girl. What are you up too?" she asked.

"Nothing just taking care of my daughter and trying to do what I have too. But how are you today mom?" she said sitting down.

"Look mom I am going to go so I will see you later I got to get these kids ready for bed." I said picking up my baby and putting Nia's jacket on and I left. When I got home I noticed that Antonio wasn't home. Again his ass is not home I don't know if I can handle this anymore. I can't stand this shit now. He asks like he can't understand hell. I just went ahead and feed my kids and get them ready for bed. When he did finally get home I knew that it was going to be a fight.

"Where the hell where you at?" I asked pissed off.

"Look you don't come to me like that first of all and second of all none of your damn business. Now excuse me." he said. I just decided to get my locks changed he will not come back in here. And I mean that.

ALICIA

Sitting with my mom is a blessing. I mean I never have a chance to see my mother that often and I live here din the same city as her. But it is not my fault. I just had some problems with my mom. "I am glad to see you Alicia." My mom saying trying to hug me.

"No mom. I still remember what happened. You trying to walk around here like nothing ever happened when you know it did. I had to take a blood test to prove that he is my daughter's father. Why? Because my mom never believed me. And I do mean never. Mom you are my mom you are never supposed to go against me but you did." I said crying.

"Sweetie, I am sorry. Look at that time I felt bad but that gave me no reason to say that you are a liar. I am sorry. But it is getting late. Take my granddaughter home." she said kissing my forehead and kissing Kia. I got up and wrapped my baby in the blankets and headed out the house. I placed Kia into the stroller and headed down the street. When I got back to my apartment my baby was asleep and I placed her in her crib and I went and started cleaning up my house. Then my phone had rung.

"Hello." I said answering the door. "Hey baby girl." my dad said.

"Hi, daddy. What are you up you to?" I said starting a load of clothes.

"Oh, nothing just wanting to come by tomorrow to spend time with you and my granddaughter." he said.

"Okay daddy well I will see you when you come over." I said hanging up the phone to finish my clothes while my baby girl slept. I was so tired I wanted to go to sleep. But being that my work wasn't done so I just turned on the television until I got all my clothes done. By the time that I got finish my little angel woke up so I had to get her changed and back to sleep.

JASMINE

After that stuff with my husband did by not telling me that my kids were with my sister had made me upset. I don't mind if she can take my boys but damn let me know I mean I am the mother of these kids and what if anything happen to my kids then what. I will be upset with my husband because he was the one that let my kids go without letting me know. I knew that I had to go and visit my mommy because I haven't seen her in a weeks and she could give me advice when I needed her. I got my kids dress and drove over to my mom's house but first I went to go see my baby sister just to make sure everything is going okay. I pulled up to her apartment and got the kids out of the car and went and knocked on her door.

"Hey big sis." she said opening the door.

"I am going to see mom today. Then, I was going to go out to dinner. Do you want to come." I said playing with my niece.

"Yeah, just let me clean up and get us dress." she said grabbing Kia.

"Alright I will be back to get ya." I said picking up my baby girl and heading back to the car. When I got to my mom's house she wasn't there so I just went back to my sister's house and waiting for her to get ready. I never saw such a clean person like my little sister. If there is a spot on the floor she is cleaning it up. But that is how we was raised my mother hated a dirty house. But when I did get back home from spending hours with my sister, my niece and my kids. I had to come home to a messed up house. OH HELL NO!

"Mommy, would you like me to help you?" Christopher asked.

"No go ahead and play baby mommy got it." I said kissed him on his head.

CHRISTOPHER

I always see my mommy cleaning up the house, cooking and taking care of us. Me, my brother Kevin, my brother Jamair and my little sister Nia. I mean my mommy does everything she makes sure we get on the bus and get to school. She also makes sure that we have clean and new clothes and shoes. This week my mommy brought us all like 2 pairs of Jordan's a piece. My dad is never home or spend any time with us like mommy does and I love my mommy and my daddy but my mommy more because she is there.

CHAPTER 2

TIFFANY

Today, I got to go back to the doctor to see what is going on with my baby. I am now 5 months so hopeful I can see what it is that I am having. I still haven't told Antonio yet because every time we talk about more kids he has a fit. Plus,he hasn't been home either for me to talk to him about anything. I am so tired of fighting with a man that doesn't want to be there. I mean hell I am a faithful woman that sits home all day and take care of my kids. Is it too hard to ask for a faithful man a man that loves me for me? I mean what I am supposed to do now that my son is starting to "daddy". What am I supposed to tell my kids? I mean do you know how bad I feel when they ask me

"Mommy, where's daddy?" It hurts me so much because I never have an answer for them. My kids love there stupid ass father. What does it take for a man to understand what they have is good until they lose it. When I laid my kids down for their naps. My stupid fiancé came into my house with another bitch. I am so pissed like right now.

"Are you serious right now?" I asked him closing the kid's door.

"You're . . . your pregnant." he said surprised.

"Yes I am but what is this." I said as he kept looking at my stomach.

"Look I came to say that we are over and I want you out of my house." he said. Is this nigga serious? I can't believe this shit. I packed me and kids clothes and got into the car and drove to my mother's house. I got up and knocked on the door.

"Baby girl, what happened? Come on in this house." My mom said. I handed her Jr and I went to lay Nia down.

"Mom, I can't believe what just happened to me and my kids." I said sitting down.

"What happened sweetie?" she asked.

"I had come back from my appointment to see if the baby is doing well. And she is but when I got home Antonio wasn't home so I just laid the kids down for their nap and as soon as I came out the room he was walking in with a girl. He told to get out mom." I said crying.

"Stop it. Stop it Tiffany I didn't raise you to cry over no damn man do you hear me. You and these kids are going to stay here until you get yourself together. You were in college when you meet this fool and what happened after you? You dropped out and got pregnant. Tiffany I have seen him beat the shit out of you time and time again. Now that you are free. Sweetie you can do everything that you always wanted to do." My mom said. I just don't want my kids to have to go through that but I got to do what I got to do.

ALICIA

My little girl just turned 6 months old today and she is looking every bit like her father. Her father came over to watch her while I went to class and work.

"Girl so how is that beautiful little girl of yours?" my best friend Lisa asked in class.

"She is so good. My baby girl just turned 6 months old today. And did I mention that her father is babysitting her today." I said finishing my work and turning it in.

"Her daddy. Girl gets out of here. Your baby's daddy got the baby." she said as we walked out of the classroom.

"Yeah but let me go and check on them before I went to work." I said jumping into my car and heading to my house. When I got there I saw the police and the ambulance at my house. I ran into the house.

"What the hell is going on?" I asked the police officer.

"Who are you ma?" he asked.

"I live here sir what is going on." I said.

"We had got a call about some guns shots and a baby getting shot." he said.

"Oh my god. Excuse me." I said running into the house. When I got in there I saw my daughter on the floor bleeding. I had a fit.

"Is she okay sir?" I said crying.

"Yes ma. Are you the mother?" he asked.

"Yes sir. I am." I said watching them put my daughter in to the ambulance. I saw my daughter father in the back of the police car. I went to the hospital with my daughter. I couldn't stop beating myself up for this. How could I trust him with her? How could I be so stupid? When my mom and my sisters rushed to the hospital.

"Alicia, what happened?" my mom asked.

"I was at school and I asked Kia's father to watch her and he shot her. Mommy, what if my baby dies. Mom what am I going to do" I said crying my mom held me tight as the doctor came out into the waiting room of the while I was on the floor crying.

"Miss Alicia Smith. Your daughter is in NCIU. She is tight for her life right now. We got the ballet out and she is resting." the doctor said.

"Thank you doctor. Thank you." I said hugging my mom. I couldn't believe that he shot my daughter. I can't believe that he would do this.

JASMINE

I can't believe that my niece was shot. How in the hell can a man shot his own child. I mean come on now. He calms that he loves my sister and my niece but then he turns around and does this. I just don't understand men. I mean they want us to be this kind of woman but and they turn out to be a whole different person. I am still pissed off that my supposed to be husband left my house so fucking messed up. I can't believe that a man can live in a house and not want to clean up but wants to bring his friends over. What the hell is wrong with him? After I have done put the kids to bed. My husband tries to come and talk to me but I really didn't want to hear shit he had to say.

"Honey we need to talk." he said as I cleaned up my house.

"I really don't want to talk to you because so much shit is being done that I don't like. And I am so mad at you for letting my kids go without telling me." I said putting up the dishes.

"Shut the hell up woman. All you do is bitch about everything. And I don't have to tell you shit about where my kids go?" he said going to into the living room and played his stupid game. I didn't say anything because that stupid nigga better believe that he is not getting none of this good tonight now argue with that bitch.

TIFFANY

Living with my mom has been a blessing and a curse. One day it's don't do that to that child and the next it's you need to teach that girl not to do that. I don't understand what she wants me to do. This child is acting up because she doesn't see her father. When my daughter don't see her father she acts like she can't listen to me but I am going to tell you one thing I am not having it because she knows what I say goes.

"Good morning mom." I said but I knew that she was a little bit mad at me because all this shit that is going down. But I don't know what else to do I am 6 ½ months pregnant with a 2 year old and a 1 year old. Today Antonio decided to bring his stupid ass around I guess he wanted to spend time with the kids. Yeah, but I wont get my hopes up high

"What are you doing here?" I asked upset with him. "Is it okay for me to get my kids for a few hours." he said.

"Now you want to be with your kids. My kids better be back here by 7pm if they are not I am coming after you. You got me." I said getting the kids ready to go with their dad. After Antonio took the kids I sat down and talked to my mom.

"Mom, what's wrong?" I asked as she sat down.

"Baby girl. I have seen you be hurt by so many men and yet you are still trying to be strong not only for yourself but for your children. All these good men in the world why sit around with a no good man. I just don't understand?" she said. My mom was right I mean there are a lot of good men in the world but why are we with these losers. I mean I know that we have kids by them but damn why we have to go through everything that they put us through. I don't want to go through this shit anymore. I am tired of it. I can't deal with this anymore.

ALICIA

As I sit in the room looking at my baby girl laying here in this hospital be I start thinking a lot about these decision that I make. I still can't believe that he had shot my daughter. I look at my daughter and worried if I can every forgive her father for that. I don't know how a man can shot their own child. I mean come on. The doctor came into the room as I sit there worrying about my daughter.

"Good morning Miss Smith." he said with a smile on his face.

"How is my daughter doing?" I asked.

"She is well. We just need to keep her in here for a few more days. But I would like to know if you would like to go out on a date with me?" he asked. I mean he is a very sexy man but I don't know if I want another man coming in the middle of me and my baby. Now that her father is in jail for attempted murder.

"Yeah, I would love too. But how about I go home and get us a picnic and eat it here with my baby because I really can't leave her side right now." I said. I knew that he liked me but I just don't want to live my child again. My mother walked into the room.

"Hey baby how you are doing?" she asked trying to make me feel better.

"I will see you later on and I will bring the stuff." the doctor said walking out the door.

"I am trying to hold on. But where did I go wrong? I feel like I let my child down. Mom, I didn't protect her the way that I should had and I just don't know what to do. I can't believe that he shot my daughter mom. She's only a month old. She could have died." I said crying.

"Come here Alicia. Look at me. I know that you are hurting baby but it was not your fault the more that you blame yourself the more problem you are going to have. Your daughter knows that you love her and that you will never let anything bad happen to her . . ." she said holding me tight. My mother had a good point but I still felt like I had let my daughter down. My mom sat by me as I changed Kia. She is awake but they still have to feed her through a tube because she can't feed herself yet but it's better than her being in that little machine and for her heart to beat or something. I still feel bad that she is on this through.

JASMINE

I can't do this shit anymore. I am tired of this man I can't believe that someone could have a family and don't want to do shit and I mean shit for them. I have to get the kids up, feed the kids, clean the house and get the kids dress plus myself. What the hell can I do? I have done asked him time and time again to help me and then he don't. Today he came in the house so fucking happy again.

"Who are you fucking?" I asked as he walked into the room.

"What the hell are you talking about? I don't know what you are talking about." he said trying to make me think that I am a fool or something. But I know he don't have to tell me anything.

"I have seen you come in this house mad and upset with the world. You don't want to touch me, kiss me or even have sex with me. Plus you don't want to do anything with your kids. Christopher always helps me clean up the house. My 9 year old son is not supposed to help me clean the house you are supposed to. How long have you been messing with her and please don't lie to me?" I said sitting at the table as the kids played in the back yard.

"I have been messing with her for a few years now. More like since we got married. I also got 3 kids by her but baby I told her that I love you and don't want to leave you. Baby I am so sorry." he begged getting on his knees.

"No. you need to go to her. So that is why you never are home when I want to be held, to be touched to even have someone to be there with me. You're just never there. And now I know why. Get out." I said.

"But babe I love you." he keep saying.

"Yeah I love you to but I want you to get the hell out of my house. And I am filing for a divorce." I said going outside with my kids. It's going to hurt them that I did that but come on this man has been cheating on me from the start. What the hell am I still doing here? It most only be for my kids cause he show me he has no love for me or our family.

TIFFANY

The baby started kicking very hard today. I don't know if I was doing too much or what but she just want to come I guess. I'm only 7 months pregnant through I don't have all the things that I am supposed to have for her.

"Mom, I think that the baby wants to come because she has been kicking really hard and pushing like she wants to come." I said not able to get up.

"Are you sure your only 7 months?" she asked looking at my stomach.

"Yeah mom but I think that I am going to go and lay down." I said just tried to get up and with my mother help I went to the room and lay down. Jr and Nia was still sleep when I went and lay on the bed with them. I tried to go to sleep but couldn't it was like I was in labor and then my water broke.

"Mom comes quickly." I said as she ran into the room.

"Okay well let me get the kids up and we will go." she said picking the kids up and taking them to the car. She rush back to help me to the car. I can't believe that I am about to have this girl right now. As soon as we passed Jasmine's house my mom ran and dropped the kid's o0ff and rushed me to the hospital. When I got to the hospital they quickly got me up to, labor and delivery. I didn't know what was going on all that I knew is that I was in a whole lot of pain.

"Ma how far is you?" the nurse asked.

"7 months" I said.

"The baby heads is out." the nurse said as the doctor ran into the room.

"Don't push." he said as I laid there wondering what is wrong with my baby.

"PUSH!" he yelled. And I did.

"It's a boy." he said showing me my beautiful little boy but that wasn't it I felt some more pain.

"Wait, don't push." he said I got worried all over again like what the hell is going on.

"There's another baby but the baby is breeched. I am going to push on your stomach to see if the baby will turn over. But if the baby don't turn we will have to do a c-section." he said. It hurt when he was turning the baby. I can't believe that I am having twins. Before I knew it the baby was out. And it was a girl.

"Sweetie I didn't know that you was pregnant with twins." my mom said so happy. I guess my sister had called Antonio because the next thing I knew that he was walking into the room with Nia and Jr.

"I will give you two a few minutes. Come on Nia and Jr. Grandma is going to take you for some ice cream." my mom said grabbing the kid's hands. After they left he sat in the chair right next to me.

"So what did we have?" he asked thinking of what the next's thing that he wanted to say.

"Twins. A boy and a girl." I said very weak.

"Oh wow twins. Listen you know that I am sorry for how things went down between us." he started as the nurse walked in with one baby.

"Wait where my other baby at is?" I asked about to have a fit and then the nurse walked into the room with my baby girl. I can't believe that I have 4 kids just like my sister.

"Tiffany I am so sorry for what had happened. I really want us to be a family so that our kids could grow up with both of us. I want to marry you I really do." he said looking at the twins. "You can see your kids but I can't be with you anymore I can't keep going through this shit with you." I said feeding the twins. I knew that he wanted to be with his kids but I just can't do this anymore. I simply mean this relationship is over.

ALICIA

I got a chance to sit with my new doctor friend while my mother sat with my baby girl. "So tell me. I know that you are angry but how could you stay with a man that don't appreciate you or your daughter." he said. I just stopped and looked at him for a while like why would you ask me something like this if you don't even know me.

"Well, I never thought about it. I always saw myself with this man. He was the first one I fell in love with when I was a freshman in high school and because we have a baby together. I always said if I was a good girlfriend that I can be maybe he will love me but I see that it didn't work like that. I never met a man that can try to kill his own daughter. I mean he always talk about how much he love his daughter but he tries to kill her. I can't respect a man like that. I mean he wanted to kill my damn daughter and I just don't know. After having a beautiful lunch I went back to the room to be with my little girl. It's a blessing that she is still living. For that I am so happy.

CHAPTER 3

ALICIA

Today my little girl gets out of the hospital. It is a blessing how much this little girl smiles no matter what her father has done to her. Tomorrow I am taking her to the see her father because I want him to see what he is missing out on. Kia has became a joyful baby and she laughs a while lot more and she plays a lot more. It is a good thing that my baby daddy didn't cause my baby's heart to turn bitter. I mean I never thought that my baby could have survived something like that but she did and I think God everyday for that. My doctor friend and yes I are getting very close he has been to my house and he has took me and Kia out to dinner and I have had sex with him already. I can tell you he is so much better than my daughters father. It's been like 5 weeks and I am staying at my mom's house with my sister and her kids. Kia's injury was very serious. I'm really going to need my mothers help with Kia.

"Mommy, we are home." I said carrying my baby girl into my room and laying her down. My mother came running into the room.

"My baby girl." she said hugging me. I guess she was tired of my pregnant sister. I can't believe that she was pregnant again. But hey that is her life.

"Sweetie you need to call your job and see if you still have a job. They kept calling and asking about what happened to the baby and everything." my mom said kissing Kia on her head. I knew that my mother might be mad if I tell her that I am taking my baby to see her father.

"Mommy, I decided to take Kia to see her father tomorrow." I said knowing what she is going to say next.

"Sweetie it is up to you it's whatever you want to do." She said. WHAT! She can't stand him but she said this. "But I don't think that it is a good idea. Why put yourself through that again. I mean come on now." She said. My mom made a good point. I don't want to put her through any more pain. I mean he did try to kill my daughter. But you know what I won't even try it.

JASMINE

I still can't believe that this man is cheating on me. What the hell am I supposed to do? I got 4 fucking kids. What am I supposed to tell them? Damn I should not have married this asshole. I can't believe that I am going through this shit again.

"Mommy where's daddy?" Christopher said walking into the room.

"I don't know baby but go and get ready for school." I said as he ran out of the room. I just don't know what to do anymore. I mean just for my son to come to me and ask that I cried. My little princess walked into the room.

"Mommy is you okay?" she asked holding my head.

"Nothing baby girl mommy's okay. Come on up here and go to sleep." I said picking her up and putting her on the bed. I know that I am now all alone. You know what I have loved this man but he never loved me. I mean when I got pregnant with Christopher I was alone throughout my whole pregnancy. And when I had him my mother was the only one there to help me. I still can't believe that I am still going through this shit with him, all my babies I had by myself. Nia was born 12 weeks early because we got into an argument and he pushed me down a flight of stairs. I look at my kids and I see all the pain that they are going through and it's crazy. But I am not going to let that stop me from being a good mother to my kids. After all the crying I did I got up and got my babies ready for school.

"Mommy can I stay home from school today?" Christopher asked.

"No, baby go ahead to school. Mommy is okay." I said fixing him breakfast while the other fights to get up.

"Jamair and Kevin come on. Let's get up." I said as I sat the bowl of cereal on the table.

"Mommy Kevin won't hurry up. Come on Kevin get out of the bathroom." Jamair said knocking on the door. Something needs to change around here in my house. I aint having it.

TIFFANY

I don't think that he understand it when I said that we are over. As soon as I was about to go home with the twins he walks in. I can't believe this shit. I don't want him to be here right now but what can I do.

"Hey are you ready to go?" he asked as I got the twins dressed and placing them into the car seat. I just don't understand what he thinks is going to happen.

"What are u doing?" I said putting the blanket on my babies.

"Look I really want to take you to the house. Please just let me take you and the babies to your mom's house." He said picking up a car seat. You know I just don't get it how a man can treat you like shit but once you give birth to his kids he changes for now. And that is what I am dealing with right now. Nia, Antonio, Ja'Nia and Ja'Mair don't need to go through this.

"CONGRADULATION" my sisters yelled when I got to my mom's house.

"Thank you. But can I get some help." I said fighting to get out of the car. My mom and Antonio grabbed the babies and headed into the house as my sisters stood at car door.

"What is it that you two want?" I said getting out of the car.

"Well, are you two backing together or what?" Alicia said holding my little niece Kia.

"Look, it's nothing like that. He begged me to let him bring us to mom's house. I can't keep going back. You know what I mean." I said moving them out of my way.

"Babe, come on I think that the twins are hungry!" Antonio yelled from the door. I could imagine how my sisters were looking.

"Yeah you two aren't together huh." Alicia said as her and Jasmine laughed as we walked into the house. I walked into the room with the twins and feed them while everyone was sitting in the living room. I am not getting back with him and that is my word.

ALICIA

I don't really care that I got fired from my job because I was missing too much days. My daughter means more than that job anyways. I mean I got like 2 pay checks to collect and now I can really focus on school I had to take a class over because I have missed to many days but you know how it is when you got a baby. I decided not to bring Kia with me to the prison to talk to her father. I can't put my daughter through anymore pain because she is too special and she doesn't need anyone else hurting her.

"Hi, Alicia. Where's Kia?" he said behind the glass.

"I decided not to bring her. But forget all the small talk why did you shot Kia?" I asked wondering if he is going to tell me the truth.

"I was trying to . . . I wanted . . . look I made a mistake I didn't mean to shot my daughter." He started.

"But why did you? All the time that we were having sex all you talked about was you getting me pregnant. And when I got pregnant you aint there for her. And on top of that you try to kill my daughter. I just don't understand what you were thinking." I said

"I wasn't thinking okay but is this what you came here for?" he asked.

"No, I am putting you on child support. And I to tell you that I got a man and he does things for Kia. And it's going to break your heart when she calls another man daddy and not you. Good bye." I said starting to get up.

"Alicia I love my daughter. I really do." He said with a tear falling down his face.

"I know you do but you have a funny way of showing it. Good bye." I said leaving. When I got into the car I cried. You know looking back I really loved him. It was our idea to have a baby but now that she is here I have to do everything. I remember growing up that my mom and dad had fights all the time but he was always trying to be there for his kids. But now that me and my sisters are older and got kids our men wants to be so different. I mean they don't want to even do anything for our kids. When I finally got back to my mom house all of my nieces and nephews were sleep and my sisters and my mom was talking.

"Kia just fell asleep do you want to go and lay her down." My mom said handing her to me. I just held her in my arms and cried.

"Sit down Alicia. See girls I know what it is that all you are going through. All three of your fathers gave a hell throughout all of your lives. But not once did I hold my head down in front of you. I stood up and took my responsibilities and raised you up to be beautiful, powerful, and great women and mothers. Now don't you let any of these men turn you into something besides what I raise you to be? Understood." My mom said. And you know what she is so right. She is really right.

DESHAWN

Look at my daughters I see me in all of them. All the pains, tears, laugh and joy. All 3 of my daughters father has hurt me so bad. I remember when I got pregnant with Jasmine her father tried to kill me and my unborn baby. I mean he would get so mad and starting punching me in the face and in my stomach. I went in 6 weeks early to have her because he kicked me in the stomach and I started bleeding. It was a good thing that my daughter came out okay and with no problems. But she had to stay in the hospital with tubes in her little mouth for about a month before I could have even held my daughter. Then about 2 years later I get with Tiffany's father and I got pregnant with her. Yeah it was kind of fast but hell he had that good good and he had put it on me. But that doesn't mean that he was a good father

34

because he wasn't he tried to be father to Tiffany until after I gave birth to my daughter. Then he just skipped town and just never was seen again. And you can just guess that Alicia's father just don't care about her either. I got those no good guys that don't give a damn about their kids and that is how my girls meet guys that don't give a damn about them either and wont take care of their children either.

JASMINE

I was so glad to see my niece and nephew. They are just so little and so cute. I remember when I gave birth to each of my bundles of joy. It is the best day that any mother can feel. As soon as I got done chilling with the family I went back home because my kids got to get clean up and ready for bed. As soon as I pulled up in the yard my husband was sitting on the steps. My kids jumped out the car and ran into his arms. I loved seeing that but I just can't do that shit. I mean he slept with someone else. When my family was telling me that he is no good for me I just stood there beside him. After he raped that girl I was the one there when his ass went to jail. I put my life on hold for this stupid ass man and he is not even grateful for it. What he does goes out and cheats on me. I got to sit there and explain this shit to my kids when they get to an age and start asking questions.

"Dad, are you coming back home? You know that next month is my birthday right dad." Christopher said.

"Me and your mom got to talk so take your brothers and sister into the house." He said grabbing my arm.

"Alright dad." Christopher said ran them into the house.

"Get your fucking hands off of me." I said pulling away.

"What is wrong with you? It's been a week now Jas. Come on baby let me back home. I miss you." He said.

"I don't think that is enough anymore. I have stood beside you when my whole family called me a damn fool and this is the thinks that I get huh. You go out there and fuck another chick and I am supposed to be there right." I said.

"Right" he said.

"Wrong? I won't do that we are over. You can see your kids but I am done with you. I can be an independent woman and I can raise my kids by myself." I said walking away.

"JASMINE YOU CANT DO THIS! YOU CAN'T TAKE MY KIDS AWAY FROM ME LIKE THIS! JASMINE!!!!!" he yelled as I closed the door. I just can't do this anymore

CHAPTER 4

TIFFANY

It has been good to be a mother again. I mean like I am already very good with Nia and A.J but now having two more babies I have to get up early in the morning changing diapers, feeding and everything I mean just doing everything all over again. I am now just getting AJ out of diapers. But you know what I love it every moment of it too. Today I woke up and looked into my babies faces. I see now that I have 4 little lives to live for and to rise into the best man and women just like their mother is. Antonio showed up once again. Damn,why can't he get the message.

"Good morning. Is Tiffany up?" he said at the door.

"Yes come on in." my mom said opening the door.

"Thank you." He said walking into the house. After I finish changing the twins I laid JA'Mair down as he walked into my room.

"Good morning." He whispered so he wouldn't wake the kids.

"Come on let's talk in the kitchen." I said laying Ja'Nia down. We walked into the kitchen and sat down at the table.

"What do you want Antonio?" I asked looking dead into his eyes.

"I want you and our kids." He said grabbing my head.

"Look, no. I can't okay. You can be a father to your kids that's all." I said pulling back my hand.

"Why Tiffany? If it wasn't for me you won't have those kids. Wait I didn't mean that." He said.

"You know what Antonio your right but now I have them and I am a damn good parent without you." I said slowly getting up.

"Tiffany, what do you mean? What I can't see my kids? Talk to me damn it." He said getting upset.

"Look, Antonio. You can see your kids. You can only be with your kids. But as for you and me we are over. I don't want you back. I just want you to take care of our kids." I said.

"No. Fine with me. Since we are done I don't give a damn about those kids. They may not be mine anyway. You raise your own damn kids." He said getting up and left. How can a man be like that? I just went back in the room with my kids. It's time to move on.

ALICIA

After listening to my mom I knew it was time for me to finish college and raise my baby. Sometimes we let men get in the middle and mess shit up for us but not me. I broke it off with my doctor friend. I decided not to let another man in Kia's life right now but he has sent me flowers and letters everyday and I know my mom is getting tired of it.

"Alicia, we need to talk." My mom said standing in my room door.

"Come on in mom." I said changing Kia bandage.

"Now this man has sent you flowers and letters. Why did you break up with him?" She asked sitting on the bed.

"Mom, I just don't want another man coming into Kia's life right now." I said feeding Kia.

"Are you sure its Kia life or yours? Baby girl you can always find a good man that can fix the pain that a bad one may have caused." She said.

"Mom, I just don't know. I thought that I had a good man until I got pregnant then everything changed." I said as a tear fall from my eyes.

"Baby girl stop punishing yourself. You are doing great. But you can't make all men the same because you had got with a low down dirty dog. Like I told you. Just be a mother to your daughter and everything will fall into place?" She said kissing me on the forehead and heading out the door.

JASMINE

I can't believe that I just did that I mean my kids has just did that I mean my kids has just keep asking where is their father and when is he coming home. It is so hard to explain to my kids as young as they are. And I don't think that I can keep on trying to put my kids through this stuff anymore.

"Mom, where's dad at?" Christopher said walking into the house from the school.

"I'm right here" my husband said walking in behind him.

"Hey dad." The kids said running into his arms.

"You all go to your room. I need to talk to your father." I said as they ran into the room. He looked at me like he knew what the hell I was going to say.

"What the hell are you doing here?" I asked picking up the kid's toys and shit off of the floor.

"I told you that you can't do this to me. I said that I loved you and that I am sorry for what I did." He said trying to make me feel sorry but it won't work. What the hell this nigga think that this shit is cool. I think not.

"Look, I said that we are done. Don't you understand that we can't go on? We can't do this anymore." I said putting the toys away. He tried very hard to keep on saying that he is sorry but he doesn't understand. How much must a bitch take before she gets tired?

"Baby. We need to talk about this." He said grabbing my hands.

"No. Please just leave. I don't want to talk about this anymore. Please get out of my house." I said trying to pull my arms. He threw me to the floor and got on top of me.

"I've tried to be nice to you but now I am going to get nasty you're not leaving me. I will kill you first. Understood?" he said looking into my eyes. I can't do shit now for real. My baby girl stood there watching and screaming. My husband got up and walked into the room. Mya ran into my arms. I just sat on the floor and held my baby tight. I know that she is scared for me but if I stay strong she will know that everything will be okay

TIFFANY

Why is it that a man would throw away there damn kids when you don't want to be with them. I never understand how a man could be so mean and stupid just because I don't want a low life nigga. As young as my kids are I am glad that they don't have to ask where there no good daddy is at. As I got Nia and A.J. ready for the tube my mom came to the door.

"Come on in." I said taking off Nia and A.J clothes and putting them into the bath tub.

"Hey sweetie. Would you like to talk about it?" She asked trying to see if I would really talk about it to her.

"Not really mom." I said about to wash them off.

"Sweetie I am here okay." My mom got both of them clean. While she did that I made them something to eat and try to get them to sleep before the twins wake up. I see that my mom had taken them out of the tube and they sat down and I feed them. As they ate the twins had started to cry. Oh my goodness I can't do this shit. I went into the room and picked up the twins and went into the living room to try to feed them as well as make sure that Nia and AJ eat so that they can go to sleep.

"Sweetie you need to talk to me about it." My mom said grabbing Ja'Mair and feeding him.

"Mom, I am good." I said burping Ja'Nia. I really see that this is a lot harder than it seems. It's a good thing that I have my mom. I laid the twins down again after the fell asleep.

"Come on Nia and Aj its time for bed." I said as I came back into the kitchen.

"Mommy just a few more minutes." Nia said

"No baby. Come on you need to lets go to bed." I said picking Nia up and putting her in the bed so that I can go and clean up the mess that they have made.

"Good night mommy." Nia said as I kissed her on the head.

"Good night baby girl. Now go to sleep." I said turning off the light and walking into the bathroom while they slept so that way I could clean up and put their things away.

"Sweetie, I am here okay." My mom said kissing me on the forehead. I fell to the floor. I can't believe that I am alone raising four kids by myself. I never pictured this for myself. I thought that I would with him forever and I guess I was wrong.

ALICIA

I started school over again today. It's been like a month since I have been in class at all. My mom decided to let Kia stay with her instead of me taking her to daycare. Going back to school is a challenge. I mean I know the material but being away from my daughter for a long period of time is a problem to me. My professor was talking today about sex and kids. I just don't know what the hell this got to do with criminal justice. This is crazy. I walked out of class as soon as I heard the bell rung. As I walked to the car someone grabbed me and dragged me into a black van and he raped me over and over again. I blacked out not knowing what was going to be next.

JASMINE

Oh my fucking goodness I can't believe what he told me. It took an hour to believe what he told me. It took an hour just to put Mya to sleep.

"We really need to talk about this." He said as I walked into the room.

"I don't want to talk to you about anything. I just want to go to sleep." I said getting into the bed.

"Look, you are going to talk to me. Or we can do something else." He said touching me.

"Stop it." I said pushing his hands away.

"Look, you're going to give me some." He said getting on top of me and touching me. He knows that if he starts kissing my neck I start giving in and that's what he did. He started kissing me on my neck and going down my chest and then to my stomach. Before I knew it he went down to my click and he started going in for the win. Oh yeah! I felt like I was just in a peaceful place. But wait a minute I just lost my mind. This man done stacked this same click and another bitches as well. And I am laying here fucking him. I must have lost my damn mind. This is crazy. I can't believe that I just did this.

"You did what" Tiffany said as I heard my nieces and nephews crying in the background.

"It was crazy I know "I said talking to her on the porch.

"I can't believe this. Come by tomorrow so that we could talk." She said. I know what that means the babies are very fussy.

"Alright I'll see you tomorrow and give them babies a kiss for me." I said hanging up and going to finish cleaning up the house. What do you do when you don't know what to do?

TIFFANY

I didn't sleep that well tonight because my mom and I sat up all night waiting on Alicia to get home. This is just not like Alicia not coming home or call. As my mom was about to call the police Alicia walked in the door. She looked like she had got into a fight. She was all dirty and just wrong.

"Where the hell have you been at?" I said pissed off.

"Tiffany, let me handle this." My mom said. She always want to give Alicia a free ride and she be doing bad shit. I just walked to my room and closed the door. I can't believe that she just got home. I can't believe that my mom won't let me get on her for this shit. I heard the front door slammed closed and my mom knocked on my room door.

"Go talk to your sister. I will watch the kids for you." she said wiping her eyes. As soon as I got outside Alicia was backing up and she had Kia with her. I walked back into the house and saw my mother on the floor. I knew something just didn't go right. I can't believe this. As soon as I was about to go and check on her I heard a baby start to cry. I ran into the room. A.J was on the floor I carried him out of the room before he woke up the twins.

"Mom is you okay?" I asked trying to get A.J. back to sleep.

"I'm fine Tiffany. Here he can sleep in my room go ahead and get some sleep before the twins wake up." she said grabbing A.J. and heading into her room. Wow, things just never go right. Alicia didn't come back to the house until the next morning but she wasn't the only one that came to the door. A white man in a nice white suit came to the front door.

"Hi, I am looking for a Tiffany Johnson." He said

"Hi, I am her. How may I help you?" I said walking up to the door.

"Well a Antonio Smith called saying that you neglect and abuse your children and you all sleep in a one bedroom." He said looking around.

"Look, sir I don't know who you are but I don't neglect or abuse my children and my kids sleep very well." I said.

"I am with child services and I am here to take your kids away from you." He said grabbing Nia.

"No. please don't take my kids." I said screaming and not letting them.

"Fine. You got 2 weeks to get a house or we will be back and we will take your kids from you. Understood." He said handing Nia back to me. I can't believe that he would do that to his own kids. He is such an asshole. It's all war now.

ALICIA

I can't believe that I am just driving with my baby asleep in the backseat. I drove to the park and just sat there for hours looking back at my daughter and wondering what kind of a life can I give her if I am still having my own problems that I am bothering with. I can't believe that I was raped and when I come home I got to deal with my mother and sister. I can't deal with it. I mean I feel that this is not the place where I need to raise Kia. If anything else happens to my daughter I don't know what I would I do. I am alone right now. I mean like what do I have to do my daughters father is in jail and I am alone by myself to raise Kia just like I have been alone I have been by myself throughout my whole pregnancy. Now that Kia is going on 3 months old and I got to be stronger than I am right now but what do I do. I want Kia to have the life that I had but better.

CHAPTER 5

DESHAWN

I don't know what is going on with my kids. Every time I see them doing good someone tries to hurt them. Why? I have no clue. People needs to stop trying to tear my girls down. They are becoming good woman even though they all got baby fathers that are not there for them or for all of my grandkids and they are the ones that are being destroyed by that.

JASMINE

I got my head all messed up I had sex with this man again now I am all confused. I never was supposed to do that. Now, look what happened shit is still the same way that it was. He goes out and comes back in whatever time he fucking wants to. And again I got to clean the house, cook and take care of the kids all by my damn self. And I am tired of this shit.

"Mommy, are you crying." Christopher said wiping my eyes.

"No baby. I am just . . . . nothing baby go ahead and go play." I said. I noticed that my husband was outside arguing with a man but I just didn't really think that they were getting louder.

"It your baby. I can't believe that you messed with my wife." The man said punching my husband.

"Hey hey please I got kids in here." I said running out side I knew it. I knew it. He done did it now. Hell no I can't do this anymore.

TIFFANY

I went out today and searched for a nice an apartment for me and my kids. You know the more I looked the messy the places were and I can't raise my kids in a trashy place. I guess I must have looked at like 20 places and I found the best one. It needs a lot of stuff in it but it's a beautiful 4 bedroom 1 bath apartment. It was clean and everything. I was really glad to find a place that I can raise my babies in. I had a little bit of money left over to get a bed each of my babies already had theirs. I am so happy because I have a place to take care of my kids. Do you know how good that feels? I wanted to talk to Antonio about what happened with him sending that damn man to my fucking house. Well, I mean my mom's house but you know what I mean. He just wants to take my fucking kids away. All the shit that I have been through with this bastard he got the nerves to try and take my kids away. Why do this shit? I just don't get it. Where did I go wrong? I just don't know.

ALICIA

I sat in my room today and just listened to Mary J Blige and rocking Kia. My mom had knocked on my room door at least a hundred times and I just turned the music up more. I really don't want to talk to anyone. I just want to be with Kia. After she fell asleep I went to put a bottle that she had in the sink so I could clean the bottles that was dirty and to make her a new one before she wakes up.

"Alicia, what is wrong with you?" my mom said sitting in the dark.

"Nothing, I got to get back to Kia." I said fixing the bottles.

"Sit down Alicia. Talk to me." My mom said.

"No mom damn. I need to get back to my baby." I said getting upset.

"Wait one minute young lady. You will not talk to me any kind of way. Do you understand me?" my mom said. I just walked off. I just don't want to talk about it. A couple of hours went by and Kia finally woke up. I am so upset that I took it out on my mom. My mom yet again knocked on the door because she heard Kia screaming.

"Come in." I said picking Kia up from her crib.

"Why is she screaming like that Alicia?" she said grabbing Kia out of my arms.

"I just picked her up damn." I said picking a oneis to put on her.

"What the hell is wrong with you? Alicia is you bleeding." She said. I fell to the floor in tears.

"Alicia, what happened to you?" My mom said sitting on the bed.

"I . . . . I was raped mom." I said looking down at the floor.

"Did you report it?" she asked.

"I can't, I don't know who it was. And plus I was in the dark truck. I need you to watch her while I take a bath. Then I will give Kia one. "I said grabbing some clothes and heading in to the bathroom. I know that she's mad now but it is not nothing that can be done. I just can't believe that things can still just be the same. I don't know why she is going to push the issue harder that it is now.

CHAPTER 6

TIFFANY

I moved into my apartment today. Nia and A.J looked to be enjoying their rooms. Even though I didn't have a lot of money but I had everything that we needed and again I am on my own.

"Nia, pick up them toys." I said walking past to check on the twins.

"Mommy, please 5 more minutes." She said dressing up her dolls.

"Alright 5 more minutes. A.J come on it is time for bed. "I said picking him up. It is so hard having 4 kids all under the age of 4 years old. Nia just turned 3 years old, A.J is a year old and the twins are now 4 weeks old. And now to top it off I am single. So I got to take care of them all by myself. And trust I got this. After finally getting A.J and the twins asleep I headed to Nia's room.

"Baby girl it's time for bed." I said seeing her putting her dolls away.

"Mommy, why doesn't daddy love us?" Nia said coming to me. Wow, I never thought that she would ask that. What do I tell her? Do I tell her the truth?

"Nia, you father loves you but mommy and daddy got thing that they got to fix." I said hoping that I wouldn't have to go through it more.

"Mommy, why? Why not?" she asked. Wow, my 3 year old daughter and all these questions.

"Mommy and daddy we love each other but we love you, your sister and brothers. But we can't be together." I said trying to explain it to her the best way I know how to.

"Now you got to go to bed." I said as she jumped into the bed and I placed the covers over her and kissed her good night. I can't believe that Nia had asked that. I had to call my mom to see what she was going to say.

"Hello." She said answering the phone.

"Mom, I can't believe that Nia asked me why her daddy doesn't love her." I said sitting down on the couch.

"Tiffany I knew that one day she was going to ask. But just keep being the good mother that you have been and as she gets older she will see that just because her father is not there that doesn't mean that you won't do good taking care of her, A.J, Ja'Nia, and JaMair. But just know that they love you." She said. I already knew that but I got to be a better mother now that I am all by myself. I sat on the phone with my mother for a while so I could clean up the house I can't stand a dirty house.

JASMINE

I KNEW IT. I KNEW IT. I knew that he was cheating again. I knew that his ass could not have been trusted. After that man left I knew that something was about to go down I had my kids sleeping in their rooms because if something happens to any of my kids I will have a fit. The man came back with a gun and started shooting up my fucking house. I had to run and protect my kids but it was to fucking late and my youngest son was shot in his head. I am so fucking pissed off right now. I started screaming and I looked and I didn't see Mya.

"Mya! Mya!" I said screaming and running through the house.

"Mommy." She cried coming from under the bed. I can't believe that she is okay. The cops came rushing up to the house. I screamed and cried when they took my baby in a body bag. As they took my husband away. I couldn't even look at him Christopher and Kevin was hospitalized for gun shots wound. I just can't believe this right now.

"I am sorry about your lost." The officer said.

"I got to plan funeral and check on my other kids. So excuse me." I said picking up Mya and getting in the car and I drove off. My mom and sisters met me at the hospital.

"How are you doing?" my mom asked me as I got out the car. I fell to the floor. I cried in my mom's arm. Tiffany took Mya back to her house with her.

"I'm here Jas. I am here." My mom said just holding me. I can't believe that my son was killed. This shit hurts so bad. I tried to get myself together to go talk to the doctors about Kevin and Christopher but I got some more bad news.

"Your son Kevin, his injuries are very bad. One of the bullets hit his lungs. And we are having a hard time with his breathing. It's like we don't know how long it is that he have." the doctor said.

"And what about my oldest son?" I asked wiping my face.

"He is in intensive care. We got his bleeding to stop. He is just in recovery. I am so sorry about your other two son's through." he said.

"When can I see them?" I asked.

"Code blue ICU. Code blue ICU." The lady said. The doctor ran off. I know that it's Kevin. How can my 2 babies leave me so soon?

ALICIA

I pulled myself together because my sister needs me. My nephew Jamair was just shot and killed and my other 2 nephew are not looking to good. I just can't believe this right now. All of these babies are being shot. I looked in Jasmines eyes and all I see is tears, anger, and loneliness. I never saw Jasmine like this. I know that when it comes down to our kids we come together. My nieces and nephews and my baby is my world and now that we have lost one its hurting inside. I walked into the room and saw my nephew gone it had shutted me down completely. This is a very painful situation. To think that my little nephew is laying here. My mom came in screaming and grabbing my nephew. I held my mom tight. Tiffany took all the kids to her house because she knew she couldn't take it right now. I wiped my tears and went into the waiting room with my sister.

"Alicia, I knew he was cheating and lying now look at my son. He is dead. And I got another baby that is not good and Chris is fighting for his life as well. I DON'T KNOW WHAT TO DO ALICIA. I AM SUCH A BAD MOTHER." Jasmine said. I never heard my sister talk like this before and now that she is I know that I got to be here for her.

"Jas, calm down. Stop trying to beat yourself up. It is not your fault that my nephew is gone." I said holding her in my arms. My sister was fighting in my arm I knew that she is just going through a lot right now and she needs me.

TIFFANY

I got all the kids tonight because I got the baddest news of my life. My sister's house was shot up and my youngest nephew Jamair was killed and now my other 2 nephews are fighting for their lives. I sat up that while night waiting to find out what is going on. I decided to call Antonio to see if he would watch all 6 of these kids while I ran up there but my mom called me instead.

"Look, I need you up here with your sisters and I'll watch the kids. I'll be there in 2 minutes." She said hanging up. I know that she can't take it. When my mom got here I rushed to the hospital. I went into the room because Jaz didn't want them to take Jamair body. She was crying and holding him tight. I had to go and grab her as they took his body away. She cried to the floor . . . Alicia ran into the room and we held Jaz. She was really not doing to good. And the doctor came in with all of us in the room.

"I am so sorry. We tried everything. Your son lungs were very messed up from where the bullet had hit him. I am so sorry. We were not able to bring him back this time" The doctor said.

"2 of my fucking kids are dead. OH MY GOD! WHAT AM I GOING 2 DO." She screamed.

"Jaz, we are here for you." We said but I know that right now it doesn't mean shit because 2 of the babies are gone. I just can't believe this shit.

JASMINE

I just found out that my son Kevin has just dead too. Now I got to bury 2 of my babies. I just don't want to talk anymore.

CHAPTER 7

JASMINE

It has been a month since I lost and buried 2 of my sons. Christopher has been out of the ICU and is starting to recover but slowly. Every day I go and see him. My husband has trial is tomorrow and even though I don't want to see his face. I got to go to the trial do for babies that was killed. I can't wait until my divorce papers come in. I can't stand his ass right now. It's because of him that my sons are gone. I have to show up to the courthouse. I really don't want to. But I need to find out what they are charging him with and how long he will be in jail. I hope forever. I might not be that lucky though. My mother took me and Mya into her house because the house was all taped up and I was not able to go back in the house right now. Mya is too young to understand what happened to her brother. But one day I will explain it to her but I just don't know when. I just want to raise my daughter and son so that won't know that their father killed their brother. So I try not to think about.

"Hey sweetie do you want to talk about it?" my mom said as I laid Mya down.

"No mom. I am good but can you watch Mya because I'm spending the night at the hospital with Christopher." I said packing a bag with some of his toys.

"You know that I will just give him a kiss for me." She said.

"I sure will. I love you mom." I said kissing her and running out the door. When I got to the hospital he was up waiting.

"H . . . E . . . Y . . . Y . . . MOM." He said. He is speaking is messed up due to the surgies that he had. I walked up and kissed him. The nurse walked in.

"Nurse, I need a word with you please." I said pulling her to the side.

"Yes ma." She said.

"How is he doing?" I asked wanting to know.

"He is doing better but we still got to work on his speaking and walking. But he is doing really well," she said. I was very glad to hear that because that means that he is fighting. As I lay in the bed beside him. He laid there and grabbed me like he never wanted to let me go.

"Sweetie, I am not going anywhere." I said. He just wouldn't let me go.

ALICIA

I started to feel very sick this morning. Like I got up 4 in the morning throwing up. I hope that I am not pregnant again. I can't deal with this hell. Kia is less than a year. I can't bring another baby in the world now. As I went to the store to get my baby some milk I picked up a pregnancy test. I had to wait until little momma went to sleep before I was able to take it. After Kia went to sleep. I walked into the bathroom and took the test. What am I going to do with another baby at 19 years old? What if it is my son? But should I keep it. All these question that kept going through my head while I waited on an answer. There it goes 2 blue lines. I can't believe it again.

"Alicia, what's . . . ? Are you?" my mom said standing at the door.

"Yes mom, I am pregnant by a man that I don't even know." I said falling into her arms.

"Baby girl what do you want to do?" she asked. I just don't know what I am going to do. But my baby didn't ask to be here or asked me to be its mother.

"I just don't know mom. I don't believe in killing my baby. I just don't know mom." I said looking at Kia.

"You have a beautiful 3 month old baby girl. I know that you are afraid about how close they will be in age. But by the time you have the baby Kia will be turning a year." My mom said trying to make me feel better but it is not working. I mean I already knew all this and it's not really helping me right now. I didn't attend to get pregnant right now. I don't know what the hell I am going to do.

DESHAWN

Damn, if its aint one thing it's another. My daughter just buried 2 of my grandsons and my baby girl is pregnant by a man that she doesn't even know. This month is just too much for me. I know that Jasmine just don't know what to do. And now Alicia is pregnant. What the hell do you do when you want to give up? I tell my girls to stay strong when I'm not.

TIFFANY

My babies just turned a month old and Antonio decides to call my phone today. Man I tell you that a man is hard to get along with sometime.

"Hello." I said while I was picking up the toys that was in the living room.

"Hey Tiff. Can I see the kids today?" He said. Hold the hell up now he wants to see my kids.

"Where at Antonio? I really don't want you coming to my house." I said.

"First of all I didn't say that I want to come to your house I just wants to see my damn kids okay. So you can calm your ass down." He said. I don't know who he thinks he is talking to like that.

"Where the fuck are you at right now. So I can bring the kids to you." I said warming up the twins a bottle.

"Come to my mom's house." He said. I hung up the phone and feed my babies. First he said that he doesn't want anything to do with my kids and now he wants to see them. This asshole. He just gets on my nerves. He really does. I got the kids dress and drove them over to his mother's house. She was standing outside. I really don't like her either.

"I want my grandkids to be with is." She said.

"Excuse me." I said locking the car door.

"Look we have tried to be nice to you but in the best of the kids we feel that they is better off with us." She said. Now I am getting pissed off and how dare they think that I am going to give my babies to them. I don't think so.

"Look, you won't get to see my kids ever again because you nor your son has done anything for any of my kids, and now you want to take my kids. I don't think so. Goodbye." I said and before I pulled off Antonio pulled up to the car.

"Why do you care Tiffany?" Antonio asked walking up. How stupid can he be?

"I take care of them. Without your help or your mothers. When is the last time any of you got my kids any diapers? How about food? Hell anything. Never so I won't let anyone take my kids." I said backing up. I can't believe this shit right now. How could I ever love this fool?

JASMINE

I decided to go to the courthouse to see the case. I really don't know if they got the man that killed my sons but I hope so. Sitting in the courtroom seeing my husband's face made me sick to my stomach. Just thinking about everything that I am going through its crazy. After the case I headed to visit Chris.

"Hey baby." I said kissing him on his head. His speaking still wasn't doing that good but just to hear him call me mommy was all I wanted. It didn't matter if he didn't know how to say all the words that he used to but just to hear him call me mommy was the best feeling. But it still hurts me to see my son in this condition. But I am glad that he is still living. I am so happy that he is fighting to do well. Every day I see that he is doing better than he did the day before. He is trying to get his strength back. By the time he gets out he will not remember what happened to him. I really don't want him to either. I just want him to get stronger for my son, my daughter and myself. And it hurts but I got to because no one else can but mommy.

ALICIA

My mom made me a doctor's appointment today. I decided to take her with me; I really want to get rid of this baby but what if this is my son or my other little girl. I am so confused I don't know what to do.

"Yes. You are pregnant. Your 4 weeks. Would you like to hear your baby's heart beat?" the doctor asked. Everything in me wanted to say no but I went ahead and said yeah. As she placed it on my stomach and I heard my baby's heart beat tears fall from my eyes. That's when I know that I couldn't kill my baby. I just can't do it. When we got into the car my mother looked at me.

"So what do you want to do?" she asked looking at me. I just don't know what I really want to do. I can't take the life of a baby that didn't ask to be here.

"I don't know mom. I heard the baby's heartbeat. I don't think that I can really get rid of my baby." I said putting my seat belt on.

"Well, I am here baby girl and together we are going to get through this together." My mom said. I was really glad that she said that because I don't know what else to do. I know that I can do it but I don't know how to raise two babies and one isn't even here yet. I am really scared.

CHAPTER 8

JASMINE

Today finally I get to bring my son home. I moved in with my mother after everything had happened. I walked into the house knowing that he is home is a beautiful but just knowing what Mya and he got to go through when they get older. Chris is 9 years old and to know that he might not remember anything from before that accident happen hurts me. I just need to get away from here for a while and raise them in a different area. I just don't want to be here anymore. I don't want to see my husband and I don't want him to see my kids either. The court gave him 12 years and the other man that they finally catch got 25 years to life for the murder of my babies. I decided to take him the divorce papers because I can't do it anymore. I won't stay in a marriage with a man that lies, cheats and involved in my son's death. I can't do it anymore. I got to think about my kids now. Mya and Chris need a mother. They need me. I am going to do what the hell I got to do to make sure that my kids have no more hurt and pain in their life.

TIFFANY

I can't believe that these fucking people got the nerves to try to take my kids. I do everything. I am the one that got to deal with 3 year old, 1 year old and 1 month old twins by myself. Getting up and feeding them, washing them, putting clothes on them. I am taking care of all 4 of my kids by my damn self and not once did my stupid ass baby daddy or his mother did shit for my kids. And all I hear from his family ask me if I need help or even a break. I mean not one. And they want to take my kids away. OH HELL NO! I don't think so. I went to my mom's house for a few hours to let her know about the shit that I just went through with him and his family. How can I try to be nice to this asshole and he wants to make it seem like I am a bad mother. Wow.

"Tiffany, I am glad to see you here today. What happened?" my mom said. She knows everything about me. It's like I can't hide anything.

"Antonio called me and told me that he wanted to see the kids. So being a good mother I got them washed and dressed and we headed to his mother's house. Soon as I got there his mother started jumping on me talking about how my kids are better being with them than me. I mean mom this nigga came in my face and said that he don't want shit to do with my kids and now they want to take my kids from me. I don't think so." I said rocking the twins in their car seat.

"Tiffany, you need to go to court and get full custody of your kids." She started.

"No mom! I don't want to do it like that. I want to do it that way. I want him to have time with his kid, but I don't want him to try to take them again. I called the man and he came and checked the house. "I said

"Tiffany, baby they is going to keep calling child services or the court to try to get my grandkids and I don't want that shit to happen.

You are a wonderful mother and I want to see you with my grandkids and not keep getting hurt by people that don't ever care about them or you." She said. I know that I damn sure that they take will not give my babies. Antonio must have lost his damn mind. If he thought he could. But I think not.

ALICIA

Finding out that I am pregnant again did come to a shock me at first but maybe it's not a bad idea. I hope that it is my little boy. I do want a little Jamair. I want to name him after my nephew that passed away. Every day I miss my nephew more and more. My sister really doesn't talk about them and I can understand why. But I think that Kia knows that I am pregnant again because she cries every time I hold her.

"Come on baby girl." My mom said grabbing Kia. My mom got her so spoil. Every time she makes a sound she is coming and getting her. It's cool to a point because she goes places and then I got time to myself. But if she leaves and don't take her then I got to deal with her little fits.

DESHAWN

Knowing that I am going through a lot doesn't mean that I am not here for my girls. It seems like Jasmine is fighting to keep her mind off of the lost of her two sons. She came out of the room today but I can tell that she has been crying all night long. Alicia,I am so worried about her. I mean she is doing the right thing but I know that she is hurting that she is carrying her rapist baby. Right now my girls need me so bad. I have never seen my girls so down like they have been these last couple of years.

"Alicia, can I talk to you?" I said knocking on the door. She really didn't want to answer the door.

"Come on in mom." she said. As I walked into the room she was changing Kia and then she laid little momma down. I knew that she has been going through it and I just want to be here for her. My daughters got to deal with.

"Alicia, have you been crying?" I said. Looking at the tears in her eyes.

"Mom, I just don't know if I can do it? I want this baby. But I just don't know if I can love this baby like I love Kia." She said. I stopped and looked at her for a minute and I couldn't believe what I am hearing coming from her mouth.

"Alicia, baby you are going to be able to love this baby just like you love Kia." I said holding her. I know that she is trying to do the right thing because that baby didn't ask to come into the world. I ended up seeing Jaz creep into the room door. And she fall beside my foot and started crying. My girls. All I can do is being here for them when they are down like this. It hurts me but I'm going to be here for them just like I am now.

ALICIA

As months went by I started getting bigger. Once again I got to go through this. I really want the doctor to find out who is my baby's father so I can press charges but instead she is going to tell me the sex of the baby.

"Hi, Alicia. Are you ready to find out the sex of the baby?" the doctor said putting that cold jelly on my stomach. I was so happy that Jasmine decided to come with me. While mom watch the kids.

"Yes, I would love to know the sex of my niece?" Jasmine said with a smile. Wow this is the first time that I seen her smile in weeks.

"Well, it is another girl." The doctor said. Oh damn. That is going to be a problem Kia already thinks that she is the boss and she is not even old enough to know what a boss is. She is only 8 months old. But I think it would be cool to have two girls. But I still wanted a boy. But I can tell that she is coming early because she is pushing herself down. I am only 27 weeks. Kia is slowly trying o come to terms with another baby on the way. She runs around like she runs things. Yes, lord she is already walking I am so happy now I am working on getting her out of these diapers. That's going to be the hard part.

JASMINE

I was very excited that my little sister asked me to go with her to the doctor today. Finding out that my sister is about to give birth to my little niece really soon is very excited. I can't wait to see her. I was very happy when my sister told me that she was keeping the baby even though she was raped. I decided to live back at home with my mother and sister because I need help right now. Christopher has gotten a little bit stronger today. He doesn't know anything that has happen still and I want to keep it that way. I decided to pull him out do school until he is fully healed. I just don't want things to get bad for him. I am glad that his dad isn't here because he would have made things a lot worst. You know sometimes I wonder where did I go wrong. I married a man that I loved that I thought loved me to. He gave me 4 beautiful kids. I cooked and clean took care of the kids. Just to find out that he has cheated on me and got another girl pregnant and 2 of my boys are died. Now everything is telling me to stop punishing yourself but I can't help it. I thought that I was supposed to but damn how much can one take? I won't let another man come in and control me and hurt me or my kids.

TIFFANY

My kids are my life. I had to go to court today because I got a letter saying that Antonio is fighting for custody of the kids. I am really starting not to like this man. I can't believe how he is trying to make me look like a bad mother to this judge. Hell he don't do shit for my kids. I am the one that does everything. I get up early in the morning. I wash them and put them to bed by 8 pm every night. I pick up their toys and stuff that they play with. It's me that does all this and not once do I receive anything from neither him nor his family and they want to come in here and talk about taking my kids. I really don't think so. He was never this kinda man. my body but my soul. I remember the man that showed his love for me instead of telling. I remember the man the man that gave me 4 beautiful kids. And now he wants to take my babies from me. This man wants to end me but it's the end of us. No more will I love a man with my soul. I can't live like this again. And I won't either.

ALICIA

I went into labor today. It started slow because once my water broke I was on 1 cm. My mother was up there with me. As Jasmine watched Kia in the waiting room. The pain was worst then how it was when I went into labor with Kia. When I had Kia it only took 2 hours. But this baby wants to be mean about coming out. 16 hours went past and I finally was ready to push. It took my 3 pushes and my little girl was out. Zakiyah Kesha Smith was born finally. She weighed 4 lbs. 2oz. She was born at 27 weeks, they had to keep her in the hospital and I cried. I didn't want to go home without my baby. Looking at Zakiyah I can tell who her father is. It Kia's fathers brother. My mom has supported me so much. Without her Zakiyah would not have anything that she needs. I love my mom she is the backbone in my life. Jasmine came into the room and brought Kia because the nurses letter me hold Zakiyah for a little while and I wanted Kia to meet her little sister. Kia got on the bed and she hugged me and then her sister. I was suprised that she wasn't mad I am glad that she is be alright. I don't think that I could never been able to handle it. I now know that being in love with a man and giving him a beautiful little girl and now I got to be a single mother of two beautiful little girls.

5 YRS. LATER

It has been 5 years and I wonder what life is now life Alicia, Jasmine, and Tiffany. I wonder how life is for the single mothers and their children.

CHAPTER 9

ALICIA

The last 5 years have changed my life. I gave birth to another little girl which I name Zakiyah. She was born 9 weeks early and she only weighed 4lbs. 2oz. It took me a month before I was able to take Zakiyah home. After Zakiyah turned 3 months old I decided to move into my own apartment but it is only 5 minutes away from my mother's house. Life has been hard trying to raise my little girls but I got through it. Kia's father got released early and he ended up calling me asking if he can come over and visit Kia. Now that she is 6 years old I guess that she wants and need to know her father. I just don't want anything to happy to my baby.

"Kia and Zakiyah. Come on babies. It time to get up." I said going into the kitchen to cook breakfast for my kids.

"I can't hear any footsteps. Come on girls." I said again. My girls don't like to get up early but they know that they have too.

"Mommy, I can't get my shirt on." Zakiyah said.

"Come here and Kia are you up and dressed." I said.

"No mommy. I don't want to go mommy." Kia said.

"Kia come on babe. Get dress." I said as Zakiyah ran into the kitchen. I do want Kia's father to see her but I know when he see Zakiyah he's going to think that I slept with his brother and it wasn't like that. ZaKiyah's father came and told me that he was sorry for what he did to me. I don't forgive him for raping me but I am not mad because he gave me a beautiful little girl but he is not allowed to see Zakaiyah. A knock came to my door a few minutes after I finish Zakiyah dressed.

"Come in." I said fixing Zakiyah plate. Kia's father walked into the room. I can't believe that's it's been 5 years and this nigga aint changed any.

"You can have a seat." I said.

"Thank you. She is beautiful." He said looking at Zakiyah.

"Thank you for coming to see Kia. Don't start any funny business this time." I said as Kia came into the kitchen.

"Hi Kia." He said getting up and walking in front of Kia trying to hug her.

"Mommy." She said running into my arms,

"So I guess you didn't tell her about me. See, this is the shit that I am talking about Alicia. Why didn't you her." He said getting pissed off.

"There was never a reason to tell her. She was too little and plus who knew when you was getting out. And plus you never did anything for her." I said.

"Let me talk to you in private." He said.

"Babies mommy will be back. Eat your breakfast." I said walking into the living room.

"Look, you fucked my brother and had a baby by him and now I am finding out that my kids doesn't even know nothing about me. Damn Alicia." He said.

"Again. I never slept with your brother. He raped me. I never attended to get pregnant again but you know what she is here. She didn't ask to be here but she is. And another thing I didn't tell your daughter about you because you shot her remember that. So don't come at me like that when you haven't been in Kia's life at all. Now excuse me I got to check on my kids." I said walking back into the kitchen. I was getting upset because I think it's like he is calling me a ho or something. I just don't know. He is still a big ass.

TIFFANY

Life is wonderful right now because I got my babies with me. Antonio decided to let me keep the kids because he knew that he wouldn't be able to take care of my kids now that they are older. Antonio don't really come by to see the kids now that he got a bitch for a girlfriend. She really don't like me because I am always calling him about our kids. Of course I am going to call him because I have kids by him so I don't give a damn about her it about our kids. Antonio and his girlfriend decided to come to A.J.'s 6 th birthday party today. Now that it's been 5 years I decided not to be mean or rude.

"Hello Antonio. Nice to see you here. A.J. your fathers here." I said walking away. A.J doesn't want to go anywhere near his father. That's Antonio fault because he never wanted to be around his kids. I guess he hated it or something because he never wanted to be because he started to make a big fuss in front of everyone.

"Tiffany, why the hell is that my kids don't want to be around me?" he said. I really don't feel like dealing with the shit on my son's birthday.

"Antonio don't start anything it's A.J's party goodness." I said trying to see if he would let it go and he just left. It really pissed me off but I didn't make it known. I can't see how a man can walk out on his kids again. After the party Nia helped me clean up but she was a bit upset

"Mommy, why do you always chase daddy away." She said wait a damn minute. I know that my 8 year old isn't talking to me like this.

"Nia go to bed before I beat you." I said trying to hold my hands back from smacking the shit out of her. She ran into the room before I smacked her. I never raised her to be disrespectful like this. And I am not having it. I wanted to go talk to her as I stand at the door I heard her on the phone.

"Daddy, I don't want to be here. Why can't live with you?" she said. Sitting there hearing my daughter talk on the phone to her father saying that she didn't want to be here with me hurts. I never imagine that Nia would choose to go to her father and leave me. And plus she disrespected me too. I went ahead and walked into the room and looked at her.

"Daddy I got to go. I think that I am in trouble. I love you too daddy." She said hanging up and walking into my arms. I can't be mad with her but I am pissed off with Antonio. After putting everyone to bed I walked into the living room to finish cleaning up. I don't know anymore. I am tired of this fucking man.

JASMINE

I never imagined that the last 5 years would be so hard because I lost my sons and now that Chris is 14 and Mya is 8 they really don't ask about their father anymore. My kids remember a lot that happened but they don't remember how Kevin whom would have been 13 and Jamair whom would have been 11 had passed away. I moved to a different house because I just couldn't live in that same house being all that my family has already been through and I don't want my ex husband around my kids. I know that he is there dad but I just dont want to see him around them. I did start dating a man. It has been a good relationship that we have been in for 2 years and he is a faithful, helping guy. I mean he help me with the kids and the house and to top it out he is a football player.

"Hey babe. I got to go on my away game so I will be gone for the weekend." He said softly kissing my lips. He is so fine, tasty, and the sex is the best. Being a football players girlfriend is a good thing until I dropped off the kids and picked up a test because I haven't been feeling that well and I hope to be pregnant. I don't want to replace Kevin or Jamair. I got home and took the test. I have no idea if I can handle another baby right now. I was happy that the test said negative. I can't say that I aint happy because I am. I do want another baby but right now. Chris is starting to act out a lot. He is starting to hang out late with some bad kids and I am not having it. I will really beat the hell out of him.

CHAPTER 10

ALICIA

Zakiyah's father decided to come and try to be a part of her life but damn it been 5 years. 5 fucking long years without a birthday card. I mean not a phone call, emails. I mean nothing. Not even a word. I can't stand his ass. And on top of that he raped me. I answered the door.

"What the hell do you want?" I said.

"Can I see my child?" He asked.

"Hell no. Get off my porch," I said trying to close the door.

"I will see her one way or another." He said. I slammed the door in his face. How dare this ass say some shit like that to me. I am the one who got and still gets up with her when she gets sick or needs to get ready for school. I mean he don't do shit but he wants to come and see her and try to play daddy. I don't think so. I went to the back door and played with me girls. I've tried thinking about dating again but my girls won't let me. Kia and Zakiyah wants all of their mothers attention and that what I am going to give them. Knowing that my kids don't really wants to see their fathers really don't surprise me. Even though I told them young their dads still haven't been there. I have been the mom and dad to my kids. Kia when she was 4 she wanted to see her father but he never answered his phone or wrote her why he was in jail. I never seen my babies cried as much as they do. And Zakiyah's father just kept denying her. I can tell that they are family. He told his family that I am a nasty slut because I got 2 kids by 2 brothers. No way in hell that he couldn't be Zakiyah's father but she looks just like him come the hell on.

KIA

My mom is the best mother in the world. I guess I don't have a dad because my mommy really don't talk about him. I love my mom she is my world. She is my hero. I love my mommy so much.

JASMINE

I am kinda glad that the test said negativity but the biggest problems that I am having is with Chris. He is only 14 years old and he comes in when he wants and now he is talking back to me. I know that he don't understand the reason why I am so hard on him but he needs to understand that it's for his own good.

"Mommy, we got to write a letter to our father for father's day and I am wondering if you can tell me something about him." Mya said

"Mya, right now mommy got a lot to do. But I will help you later okay." I lied not knowing what to tell her. Than my grown ass man walked into the door.

"Come here." I said he tried to work past me. I know that the power to beat the shit out of him but I won't because I can't become that kinda mother.

"What?" he said. I feel like wanting to beat his ass but I didn't touch him.

"Where have you been at?" I said trying to be so damn nice but he is testing me so much.

"Mom, look fall back you're always getting on me." He said. You know what I just walked away. Some parts of me makes me the mother that I am and some makes me wants to beat the hell out of him.

TIFFANY

Sometimes I wonder why I got with Antonio. I guess at that time I just wanted a fine man. I did get and I got 4 kids to go along with him. Don't get me wrong I love my kids but I can't stand his ass. How can he not be here for his own child's party. I mean he hurts my kids and they love him so much. I am the one that got to sit up and hear them cry all night long. I can't believe that Nia stood up to me like that. Antonio decided to finally call me.

"Hello." I said sitting in the living room.

"Look, I don't like the way that shit went down at A.J's party. I don't know what you told my damn kids and I am know what you told my damn kids but I really am not happy about it." He said mad as ever.

"Look, Antonio I don't have time for this you're putting a bitch in front of your kids and now you want to come at me like you're a fool. Hell to the no." I said. I know that we will start arguing and that's what happen. I get so tired of hearing the same stuff over and over again. I mean damn how much can a mother take. After hanging up with him I just cried. I feel like I'm not the mother that I want or need to be yet but I am trying so hard to get there. But how much pain can I go through.

CHAPTER 11

ALICIA

Zakiyah's father family is requesting that I get a blood test done to prove that he is the father. I can't believe that I got to keep going through this again. Zakiyah and Kia came into my room and sat beside me on the bed.

"Kia, what's going on in school?" I said holding Zakiyah in my lap.

"Nothing mommy. I made a new friend today." She said coming closer to me.

"And you Zakiyah." I said as she smiled in my face.

"Mommy, it's great." She saiding laughing hard. I have 2 wonderful girls. These girls are my heart. As I look at my girls play I see that this is my life now and I won't change it. I waited a week for the blood test to come back and it was positive that he was Zakiyah's father. He decided to bring his fake ass to my house. As opened the door I wanted to knock him the hell out just for coming to my house.

"Yes how may I help you?" I said standing in front of the door.

"Can I see my daughter?" he said. That's what pisses me off about him. One minute he don't want to see her and the next he do want to be bother with her and I don't understand him.

"I guess. Where is your brother." I said.

"I'm right here. Can I see Kia?" he said. Damn what is going on? I mean everyone wants to see their kids now that blood tests proves it. I don't even know how they are going to take this. I decided to let them in.

"Kia and Zakiyah come here please." I said sitting on the couch. Kia and Zakiyah ran into the living room.

"Girls, your fathers wants to see you." I said. I know that it's not too late for John and Shaun to be in their children lives. My girls walked so slow like they didn't want to be near them. I don't blame my girls. Not one bit.

JASMINE

Mya still continues to ask about her father and it's crazy. I really don't want to tell her about him. She only knows that she has a mother and that's how I want it to stay. It might be selfish but this man never did anything for these kids. I want it to stay to that way. I received a phone call from my ex husband today. I don't even know how he got my number.

"What do you want?" I said not wanting to talk to him at all.

"Jasmine, I am really sorry. And I really want to see my kids please." He said.

"How did you get my number?" I asked I know that he wouldn't tell me but all I know is that I am pissed off that he called me house.

"Jaz please let me see my kids." He said again

"Hell no. How dare you call me and ask me something like that. You know that it is not going to happen. Look, it's not a good idea for you to call my house so please don't call me house again." I said hearing my mother voice in the background. I can't see myself letting him see my kids. After everything that he has done. I would be a fool. Nope won't and cant. After hanging up Chris finally decides to come home. But he is all bloody up.

"Chris, what happened to you?" I said getting up off the couch and walking to him.

"Mommy, I am so sorry. I have been disrespecting you and stuff. I should have listened when you told me things. I am sorry." He said hugging me.

"Again Chris what happened?" I said looking at him.

"I got into a fight with some gang members. I was supposed to join and I backed out so I got beat up for it." He said.

"Boy, are you crazy. You shouldn't be trying to get into a gang. Your smart than that baby." I said.

"I know mom and I am so sorry." Chris said hugging me. Maybe it's my fault why he wanted to join a gang. I kept him in my arms for a long time I can't imagine losing anymore of my kids.

TIFFANY

Today I decided to spend the day out with my babies. I love spend time with Nia, A.J, Ja'Mair and Ja'Nia. Knowing that Antonio doesn't want to be in my kid's lives hurts me a lot. Have you ever tried struggling to raise kids knowing that there is no man around to make my sons into men?

"Mommy, is daddy coming to see us today?" A.J asked over and over again.

"I don't know baby. But I will ask him and see." I said. I know that I might not be able to get him to watch them for a couple of weeks or even a couple of days.

"Antonio, your kids would like to spend a few days with you." I said trying to see what he might say.

"Yeah, I would love to get the boys for a couple of days." He said.

"And what about the girls?" I said wondering what smart shit is going to come out of his mouth.

"If I had to I sure will. Look, Tiffany just have them ready in 5 minutes. All 4 of them." He said.

"Thank you." I said. I ran upstairs after hanging up and pack some outfits for the kids. I know that A.J would be happy but I don't know about my girls. Antonio showed up like 10 minutes later alone. He don't really look very well.

"Antonio, what's wrong with you?" I said letting him in.

"Tiffany, I need to talk to you. Can we have a seat?" he said looking very sick. I mean I never seen him like this before. And to top it off he look very olds and just nasty.

"What wrong Antonio?" I said getting very scared.

"Look, I just found out that for the last 2 years I have out that I has diagnosed with cancer. And it's hard now. I got to start chemo and my girlfriend left me when she found out that I have cancer." He said. I really wanted to feel bad but now. He have hurted me so bad. But it's like he's trying to be a man. I guess.

ALICIA

Seeing my kids laughing and playing with their father was the most beautiful thing that I had ever seen. Kia and Zakiyah ended up falling asleep in their dad's arms. After putting the girls to bed they came into the living room and wanted to talk to me. Wow, now they want to communicate.

"Alicia, look I am sorry that I had raped you but I am so happy that you gave me the best thing that no other woman can. Zakiyah is the best thing in my life right now." John said. I guess him saying sorry is supposed to make me feel better. It does. I never found a man that would say that they are sorry. And all Shaun says is that he wish that he would have had more of a relationship in Kia's life before and how he is so sorry for hurting me and Kia. I mean it felt good to hear them say the things that they are saying. After they left I walked and stood in the girl's room just to make sure that everything is cool and they are sleeping like the princess that they are. The next morning I decided to go and visit my mother. I got the girls dressed and I headed to my mom's house. When we arrived I saw her growing something in the yard.

"Hey mom." I said getting Zakiyah out of the car.

"Hey babies. Come and give grandma some love." She said getting up and dusting herself off. The girls love their grandmother. I haven't been over her in a while because I just been trying to get my household together. The girls ran into my mom's arms. After she finish hugging them we walked into the house.

"Alicia, I haven't seen you in a long time." She said washing her hands and finishing the food on the stove.

"Yeah mom. I have been getting the girls good with school and getting my household together." I said getting something cold to drink. The girls went into the room and played. I can tell that my mother missed me because she kept hugging me.

DESHAWN

I haven't seen Alicia and my granddaughters in like a month. I was surprise to know that she had come over. The girls are getting big and are so beautiful. To think that Alicia was saying that she could not raise two little girls she had did a hell of a job. They came out wonderful. I can't begin to tell you how much better Alicia looks. She has really taken care of herself and I am so proud of her.

"So Alicia, have a seat and talk to your dearest mother." I said taking a seat.

"What's going on mom?" she said laughing at me.

"How have you been?" I asked knowing from the way that she looks she's doing wonderful.

"I am wonderful. You know that John and Shawn both come and spent time with their kids. It's cool mom that they want to see the girls." She said. I never see her happy. Just by being a year apart they pay and laugh together the way my kids used too. I really haven't seen Jasmine since she moved but I understand because these girls are now women that have lives and kids of their own. I enjoy seeing my girls being the woman that I have raised them to be. I don't have anything to worry about.

JOHN

Sometimes the ones we hurt the most important person in our lives. Someone that gives us something special and my daughter is very important to me. Looking into her eyes I could see the pain, tears and hurt that I had put her mother through. Sometimes you can't take back the pain but you try to make it better. And I am fighting so hard to. For the last 5 years I have missed so much. Her first tooth, her first word, her first walk, I mean everything. It hurts me so much just to know that I missed so much.

SHAWN

Seeing Kia again was a very good thing. I missed a lot of her life and I can't understand why I was so stupid. All 8 of my kids I have seen and did something for but I don't want to be in my youngest daughter's life. I feel like a no good man. A dog hell I love Alicia. I love her a lot but I just don't know how I let her go and I feel so foolish. Now she is gone. It's crazy how a man can treat a woman like dirt. I guess that I didn't know what it was like to be a man until I had to live without Alicia. I am regretting every single night of my life. That's not the kind of person I wanted to be I wants to be a great father and husband and one day I will. I hope.

JASMINE

I hope that Chris learned his lesson about being in a gang. I tried to make sure that he's in the house at a reasonable time. My boyfriend came back home today. I was so glad to see him and the kids was as well. My kids loves him so much. He has been there for them since he has been in my life. I walked into the room to tuck my little one in the bed.

"Mommy, I love you "Mya said handing me a book.

"I love you too but what's up?" I said sitting on the side of the bed.

"I was just wondering why you don't talk about my daddy." She said. I know that it was coming. I don't want them to know about him. It's not like he will do anything for them anyways. And plus he did things that I want to forget. Mya and Chris is living the life that I want to and the life that they deserve. At times this the way that I want it to stay and most time it didn't know.

TIFFANY

I decided to let Antonio stay the night on the couch. I am not trying to get back with him but I want him to spend more time with his kids. As I finished cleaning the kitchen he placed the babies down to bed. I was surprised when he came to see if I needed any help damn this man never wanted to help me before.

"Tiffany, thank you for letting me stay here with you and the kids." He said I picked up the toys on the floor. I know that he is sick but he is trying to be very nice but he really asked to help me out. Wow, this man is really trying to change. I made the couch up so nice so that he would be very comfortable. As he went to sleep I went into my room and just thinking about everything. He is sick and I want to be honest with my kids but I don't know what words to say. I don't want know how to tell them. I don't want to get with Antonio but the love is still there. The next day I left stuff for my kids. I saw my mom in the store to my surprise I haven't seen me mother in like some months so I decided to call her out.

"Hi, mom." I said running into her arms.

"Hello Tiffany." She said hugging me. It was just a beautiful feeling. I felt so good.

"Why are you so happy today?" she asked me.

"Antonio's back." I said smiling.

"Okay." She said.

"He needs me mom." I said pushing the cart through the store with my mom. I know what she is about to say.

"Don't get hurt baby." She said. Wow, I can't believe that's all that she said. That's so crazy. I picked up the things that I needed and I headed home. When I got home Antonio was outside playing with the kids. I am so surprised. It's great. But surprising.

ANTONIO

You know that it takes a man a long time to know what they need to do and who they really love. I really do love Tiffany and I want to be with her but I bruised her heart so bad. Sometimes you don't know how much you love someone until you can't get back with them. I can't believe that I have missed so much. I am a good man now and until I die I am going to be a great father to my kids. I want to marry Tiffany. I really do. But as much as I put her through I don't know if she would even go back out with me. Every night I pray that she would be with me. I have changed and I hope that she sees it.

ALICA

I decided to stay the night at my mom's house because I really didn't feel like driving from my mom's house because my little girls are asleep and it is hard to wake them girls up. My mom had let the girls sleep in my old room. The same room that I raised Kia in. I was surprised to see them sleep together like that. I remember doing this with my sisters. We used to cuddle together.

"What's wrong Alicia?" my mom said as I stood at the door looking at my girls sleep.

"Nothing. Just watching my girls." I said as my mother walked up behind me.

"I remember when you were younger. You was just like them but now that you are 24 years old I have seen the woman that I love and respect. You have really turned your life around Alicia." She said.

"I had to mom. Kia and Zakiyah needed a mother. And I knew that's what I had to become." I said. I always knew that I had to grow up if not for me for my girls." I said but I never knew how much I grew up in 5 years. My kids made me the woman that I am now. I wanted to call my doctor friend again. I don't want to replace my kid's father but I want my girls to have a father. Plus, I am ready for a 3rd child. Shawn and John can always see their kids.

CHAPTER 12

JASMINE

Chris and Mya are getting ready for Thanksgiving but it's not for another 3 weeks. I decided to talk to my boyfriend to see if he would call his family and kids to see if they wanted to come. It means a lot to me if his family come and be with me and my kids. Now that my kids are asking about their dad I want him to make them feel wanted something you know.

"Honey, how it went." I said watching him hang up the phone.

"They aren't coming." He said feeling bad.

"It's okay. It's fine. If you want to go be with them." I said trying to be understanding.

"No they aint coming because they want us to come to them." He said playing me.

"Are you serious?" I said jumping into his arms.

"Yep. They can't wait to meet my family." He said. Damn I love hearing that. I got a complete family again. Even through these years have gone by I still miss Jamair and Kevin but I know that my babies are happy and in a much better place. One day I will talk about what happened to my babies but right now is not good.

TIFFANY

Slowly, I see Antonio turning into the man that I always wanted him to be. Seeing, the kids laugh and play just having a good time with their father melts my heart. What do I do it's like I want to be with him but then I don't. How can I love someone and not understand what position my heart is in, like I feel something for him but I am trying not to get hurt again because I really can't take it.

"Come on kids time for dinner." I yelled outside. They ran into the house and walked towards the bathroom. As Antonio came into the kitchen.

"Need some help?" he said. Wow, he asked again.

"No just go ahead and have a sit with the kids. I got this." I said putting the food on the plates. I set the food on the table. I really didn't feel like eating. So I went into the room and tried to clean up. After everyone ate I sent my kids to bed. My kids were so tired they fell right to sleep.

"Tiffany, can we talk?" Antonio asked.

"Yeah. I guess that we can." I said sitting down on the couch next to him."

"I know that I did you wrong and I am so sorry for that but I really love you and I want you to be my wife. I would love to be your husband." He said. I sat lost for words never before he wants to be my husband and now he does. I really don't know. I love him I really do. How is it that a man can hurt you and then come back 10 times better? I just don't know what to do. I want my kids to have their father but I just don't have a clue about me and him.

CHAPTER 13

ALICIA

I walked into the store with Kia and Zakiyah trying to find something to cook.

"Alicia." A man said from behind. As I turned around I noticed it was my doctor friend. Damn, after 5 years he is still looking good as hell.

"Hey how are you?" I said as Zakiyah pulled my jacket.

"I'm good. I see you got 2 beautiful girl now huh." He said smiling with his perfect white teeth damn.

"Yes of course you remember Kia. This is my baby girl Zakiyah." I said smiling with nasty thought going through my head.

"Would you all like to have dinner with me?" he asked. Hell yeah!

"Yes we would." I said finally picking Zakiyah up.

"See you at 8 then." He said walking off. Oh my goodness. He is still so fine still I can't believe that he asked me out.

"Mommy, he is fine." Zakiyah said hugging me.

"I know baby." I said. I could look in Kia's face and see that she was not please with it. O just doesn't know why she wouldn't want a good father figure in her life.

"Mommy, I want to go to daddy's house." Kia said.

"Your father is busy." I said

"No I WANT TO GO TO MY DADDYS HOUSE NOW." She yelled. Wait I know that she is not yelling at me. I know like hell she is not yelling at me. I've tried it the nice way but let me try it the mean way.

"Kia you're not going and if you yell at me one more time I will beat your ass." I said pushing the cart. She started screaming and yelled in the store. I just don't know what to do. She is really showing her ass. I don't know what to do so I had to go and talk to my mom.

"Mom she just went off. She started screaming and everything. I just don't know what to do." I said hoping that my mother can tell me something.

"Alicia, sweetie I just don't have any idea. She doesn't want another man to take her father's place." My mom said.

"Mom, he won't I want let that happen. My babies will always have their father. Well, go talk to my daughter." I said getting up. I still mad at Kia for acting like that I am going to give her a chance to listen to me.

JASMINE

3 More day until we head to my boyfriends family's house for thanksgiving I can't wait. I am so happy. I haven't told Mya and Chris

yet. But I will I just don't know when because I don't know how they are going to handle it. Chris has started to change his ways. I don't know if I want to tell him about this father. I know that his father is in jail. I had got pregnant with Chris before I met my ex-husband. But I want to wait until he turns into a man.

"Mom, you need some help." My baby asked me.

"No but thank you Chris but I do want to talk to you." I said sitting down at the table. I have to do it because I can't lie to my child.

"What's wrong mom?" he said sitting next to me.

"I know you been wanting to know about you father right." I said seeing him getting mad.

"No mommy, I don't want to know. I am good. I got you." He said giving me a kiss and heading into his room. Wow, I can't believe my baby. Chris doesn't want to know his father and I don't want to bring it back up until he wants to talk about it. I finish cleaned up and I went into my little Angels room. She was still awake. She wants to know about her dad but I feel that she is too young. Mya is only 8 years old.

"Mya, you got school in the morning." I said sitting on the edge of the bed.

"I can't sleep mommy." She said playing with her dolls. She lay in my arms and I played with her hair. My kids are my world. They are the reason why I love.

TIFFANY

It's been a couple of days since Antonio asked me to marry him. And still hasn't answered him yet. I just don't know. I do love him I really do but am I'm not ready to get back with him. It's bad enough he is sleeping on my couch and I aint going to lie. The first night I did have sex with Antonio. Hell, I was feeling bad for him. But I just don't want mix feelings.

"Tiffany, are you going to give me an answer?" he asked as I cooked breakfast for the kids.

"I don't want to have mix feelings Antonio. The things you did to me before. I just don't know what to think." I said.

"Baby, I will never hurt you again. I have changed." He said grabbing my arm. I always remember how abusive he used to be. I don't know. He may look different, talk different and act different but I don't know I tried to see things in a different view but I . . . . I don't know I am so confused.

"Tiffany, I know you are scared but I love you. I was a fool when I was younger and I am trying to make it up to you, I just don't want to leave this world without making the woman that I love my wife and baby that is you. Marry me." He said getting on one knee. Damn, I just don't know I am so confused man. I left him and slept with him. And now he wants to marry me. I just don't know what to do it will be good for the kids. Its just like I don't think that . . . . I don't know what the hell do I do?

ALICIA

I decided not to go and talk to Kia. I dropped her off at her father's while I went out on a date. Zakiyah wanted to stay with my mom. My doctor friend came and picked me up. He still just as fine as hell. I tried not to keep looking but I couldn't help it. I couldn't stop thinking about my girls. As he was preparing the meal my phone ringed.

"Hello. What . . . . Where are you? I'll be there in a minute." I said pissed off.

"Where are you going? What's wrong?" he asked.

"My baby." I said. When we got to the hospital I was pissed the fuck off.

"Mom, where is she?" I said running up.

"In my private area. He put something inside of me and it hurted mommy." She said crying. He raped my child. The doctor came and pulled me outside.

"Ma, your daughter was raped. And she was bleeding internal we did stop it but we are going to have her stay for another day." The doctor said.

I can't believe this shit he is crazy. He raped my daughter. I waited a little while before I went back into the room with my baby. How is it that I gave this nigga a chance again and he did shit again. What the fuck? I can't keep going through this shit or putting my daughter through this shit either. First, he shot my baby and now he raped her. What? I just don't know what the hell to do. I am sick and tired of keep putting Kia through this shit. I finally went back into the room with my daughter. I feel like a bad mother. I can't even protect her or keep her safe. Damn, I am so tired of feeling less of a fucking mother, when I went into the room she was crying. Kia was so afraid that I was mad with her.

"Mommy, I am so sorry." she said with tears pouring down her face.

"Baby girl, you have nothing to be sorry about." I said wiping the tears from her eyes.

"Mom, I didn't mean to be rude." She said.

"Kia, your my daughter you are just like your mother. I love you baby. I am sorry that I haven't protected you like I should have." I said holding Kia in my arms. I feel so bad. What am I to do now?

CHAPTER 14

JASMINE

Today is the day that we leave to head out to my boyfriends family house and my ex husband came knocking on my door. I can't believe that this asshole is standing at my door. I am so pissed off.

"Jasmine, I want to see my kids." He said as I placed the suitcases in the car.

"I don't know how the hell you got here but you need to go." I said.

"Hell no I want to see my kids." He said as my boyfriend walked out the house.

"Jasmine who this?" he asked walking up beside me.

"My ex-husband baby." I said. I could tell that my boyfriend was pissed off.

"Yo man, get the hell away from my house." He said.

"Jasmine, I want to see my kids." He said walking off. As we got into the car we drove to go and pick up the kids from school. He just wouldn't say a word to me. He is just so pissed off. He must think that I brung that ass to our house but I didn't. I didn't even know that he knew where we lived at. When Mya and Chris got into the car I looked at him but he wouldn't look back. After 6 hours of driving I turned around and saw my kids sleep so we stopped at a hotel so that we could get some rest.

"I am not mad." he said but I could still tell that he was so I started kissing him on his neck and unbuttoning his shirt. Before I got to the last button he picked me up and laid me down on the bed. Damn, he started kissing me on the neck and undressing me. I think I love sex when he is mad because he does shit that he would do if he isn't pissed. He went down my body kissing and licking and then the rough sex began. I thought that the room was going round in round because it was like we haven't had sex in months. I was glad that the kids were in the next room because I mad so much noise that everyone could hear us. In the morning a big smiled came over his face as if I brighten up his life or something. But I could still tell that he was not over the fact that my ex husband was at our house. As we got back on the road. I looked at my babies. They sat in the back sit and were so happy. It was like everything that they had been through in their lives you can't even tell because they are happy joyful kids and that's the part that love. I started feeling that I wanted to throw up.

"Baby can we stop I really don't feel well." I said. As soon as he pulled over I ran out the car and threw up. I really don't feel well. I think that I am pregnant again. This is the same way that I felt when I had all my kids except Mya. I didn't know that I was pregnant until I had her.

TIFFANY

Tomorrow is thanksgiving and I am glad that Antonio is here to be with the kids. I started cooking starting with my desserts. Nia ran into the kitchen.

"Mommy do you need some help." She said.

"No thank you baby. Go ahead and have fun." I said. I still don't believe I have a man that I couldn't stand wants to be my husband. It's hurting me because I really do wants to b e his wife but I am so scared because I don't want to be hurt again. He can say it 5 hundred times that he wouldn't hurt me but I just don't know. I noticed that he has been looking very sick lately.

"Antonio can we talk please." I said calling him in from outside.

"Sure, I will be back kids play nice." He said coming into the kitchen.

"Listen, I love you I do and I always will but I don't think that we should get married. You can stay here as long as you like to but I can't marry you. I am sorry." I said but the look on his face was not pleasing. I just don't know what to do. I love him I really do but I don't know what to do. I . . . . I know that he is pissed.

"I don't understand Tiffany. I love you and I want us to be a family. Damn, did you think about our kids before you made your decision? Huh do you ever think about what is good for them or is it always about yourself. Hell I came back as a man and said that I am sorry and I got down on my knees twice and asked you to be my wife. I madly I'm love to you so preciously and you are telling me that you don't want to marry me. Girl something is wrong with you." He said.

"Antonio, it's not like that and I do think about my kids every day. Who do you think about? Did you think about when you did all that. When you didn't want shit to do with my babies? I feel think that we should just be parents for our kids that it." I said.

"Why Tiffany?" he asked.

"Look, it's just not a good idea." I said as he walked back out the door. I can't believe that he doesn't understand. I just want us to be parents. Damn, is that asking too much. My babies deserve to know who their father is.

DESHAWN

This is the first thanksgiving that I am not going to have any of my kids and grand's with me. Alicia is going through that bastard raped my granddaughter. I just want to kill his ass. Kia just keeps going through stuff I don't think her father knows how lucky he is. I mean she is a very bright little angel that loves her father but what kind of father would hurt their daughter the way that he does. But Alicia needs to stop putting these kids through this shit. I am not saying that it is her fault but I know that she needs to stop letting these kids get hurt. Tiffany, she got her ex living with her and now he wants to get married and Jasmine. OMG I just don't know what to do.

ALICIA

The doctor decided to let Kia come home today and my mom brought Zakiyah to the house. I am glad that I have full custody of my girls because I will not let anyone else hurt my babies I put that on everything that I love. Kia fell asleep as soon as I got her home. My mom was very pissed when I came back downstairs.

"Alicia,I should beat your ass. How do you still let this man in these girls life?" she said.

"Mom,I thought that he had changed. It not like I knew that he would fucking hurt my baby like that damn." I said falling into the chair. I looked at Zakiyah as she came and sat into my lap.

"First, watch your mouth because I am still your mother and second of all you are a good mother but you letting a no good man and I do mean a no good man hurt your daughter." She said.

"I just don't know anymore. I was just trying to give my kids what I didn't have. A father. I thought that I was doing the right thing. I want my girls to know who their fathers are." I said feeling bad. After my mother left. I carried sleeping Zakiyah to her bed. As I laid her down I looked at my daughters. And I kissed them on their heads and went downstairs because I heard the door bell ring but I prayed before I answered the door. Lord, what am I going to do I need your help to protect my babies I can't do it without you. I am so scared because I am doing the best that I can to be a good mother and it feels like I am failing.

"Hey come on in." I said letting my doctor friend come into the door.

"Are you okay?" he said walking into the door and walked to the couch.

"No. He raped my daughter. How can I be okay when my little girl is in so much pain right now. It is all my fault." I said tears rolling down my face.

"Baby it is not your fault. You didn't know that he would do it. Listen you know that you want to punish yourself but don't baby. I am here for you. I will help you these times because I know that you need someone that you can trust." He said holding me. I never met a man that can tell me the truth and make me feel good about myself the way that he do.

JASMINE

We finally pulled up to my boyfriend's parent house. I really don't feel good. I know it is a possible that I can be pregnant again but I hope not. As we got out the car his mother walked out the door. She was so beautiful. She looked right in my face and said.

"Your pregnant." She said just looking at me. Wow, how can she look at and tell something that I really don't so.

"I don't think so." I said. But I could tell that my words didn't make her happy.

"Mom, this is my girlfriend Jasmine and our kids Mya and Chris." He said.

"Hi, how old are you guy?" she said looking at them with a big smile on her face.

"I am 14 years old." Chris said.

"And I am 8." Mya said. I looked at my kids as they played around with the other kids. I was so happy to see that I walked into the kitchen to see if I could help. His sisters and mother was cooking.

"I see that my brother loves your kids." His sister said.

"Yes and they love him too. He has been a great father to them. Plus he helps me the way that I needs to be help/" I said watching him play with Chris and Mya.

"So how into my son are you?" his mother asked.

"I love your son. His everything that my ex husband couldn't be. He brightens my life as soon as he walks into the door. I am in love with him." I said.

"Yeah so are all the other girls that were with him. Are you just with my son for his money?" she asked.

"No ma. I love your son for the kind of man that he is. I want to marry your son and spend the rest of my life with him and only him." I said seeing a smile come over her face. She knew that I was telling the truth. After preparing the food I called Chris and Mya in so they could wash up for dinner. I wasn't feeling so good so I went and lay down for a little bit. My boyfriend let me sleep for a little while then he got me up so that we could go for a walk in the park so that the kids could play and we could talk.

"Honey, you know that I love you. And I do whatever it takes to be with you forever. Would you marry me?" he said on one knee.

"YESSSSS!" I said jumping into his arms. I pray that this marriage last. The only thing that is left is to tell him that I might be pregnant. I know that I am so before we went home he stopped at a gas station and I went in and grab a pregnancy test. We arrived back at his mother's house and I made Chris and Mya lay down for the night and I took the test. My boyfriend had no idea what I was doing until 15 minutes later when I came out the bathroom smiling holding the test.

"AM I?" he said smiling

"Yes we are having a baby." I said as he ran to me and picked me up. I never saw a man get this happy before. I mean my ex-husband didn't act like that when I became pregnant with any of our kids. It feels good to have a real man that loves you the way the he do.

CHAPTER 15

TIFFANY

Antonio really didn't want to talk to me at all today. I guess the point about us not getting married pissed him off. He just needs to understand. I am not alone in this situation I have to think about my babies as well. Don't get me wrong he is dying and it is really hurting me inside but I can't put myself in the same situation that I did 5 years ago it wouldn't be fair to my kids or myself. Sometimes a woman is used to letting a man come in and turn their lives around but not me. Hell, I am a mother and I don't want my daughters growing up letting any man come in and beat on them like I let their father do to me many times before. My girls seen enough of that when they were little. Don't get me wrong I love Antonio. He gave me the best blessing that any woman can ask for. My 4 beautiful babies. Every day I look into my kids face and I see Antonio. A.J is his twin. He is a joyful little 6 years old with a smile that would bright up your life. Nia is just like me and her father. She is my little 8 year old lady. She is so sweet, calm and just a bundle of joy in my life. And my twins are too much. But they are my angels. Maybe because my kids only understand that daddy is back and that's all they wanted. It is so confusing for me. I have mix feeling in this situation. I just want my kids to grow up without any problems in their lives like I did. I am fighting so hard for my kids to have their father because I never had mines and growing up it hurted me and I don't want my kids to feel that same pain. I don't want Antonio mad at me. I think that it is best that we stay where we are as friends and parents because it's very important for our kids benefit.

ALICIA

I didn't sleep all night because I was beating myself up. Kia slept only for a few hours before she got up crying and shaking. I heard her tossing and turning all night. I knew that she would wake up Zakiyah so I brought them both into my room. I held Kia in my arms hoping that she would stop crying but it didn't work.

"Baby girl mommy got you. Calm down I won't let anyone else hurt you won't I promise." I said. I sat up all night trying to wait for Kia to go to sleep. I think it took me a half of the night to get her to sleep then Zakiyah woke up throwing up so I really didn't sleep at all. I had to clean my baby up then put new sheets on the bed. We just lay on the couch downstairs. I finally managed to get Kia and Zakiyah asleep and I went to sleep at 9 in the morning. I was surprised that we slept half the day. I heard the doorbell rung at least 5 times and my phones went off but we didn't move. My mother came by and she said that she was going to stay the night so she could help me with Zakiyah and Kia. These girls are a handful with one is sick and one crying all night no one gets any sleep. The next morning I woke up to the smell of breakfast. I really didn't get to sleep last night until late because Kia would go to sleep again so I held her in my arms rocking her to sleep the whole night. My mom had Zakiyah but when I woke up Zakiyah was in the bed with me. My girls are used to being in the bed with me when they are sick because if not they will have a fit. I was glad to hear that Kia's father had got 25 years for raping a child and I found out that Kia was not the only one of his kids that he did that to and I see why the mothers told me not to let Kia by him. But he lost that and it will never happen again. I promise you that.

JASMINE

Being pregnant is a total shock but then again it isn't because I knew all along that I was pregnant but didn't want to admit it. To see my fiancé this excited makes it a lot easier. I know that he is going to be a great father because I see how much he loves Chris and Mya. They are his world and if Jamair and Kevin was here he would had love them too. I love being a mother on some days it is hard and some days it's the best feeling in the world. I called Mya and Chris into the room to tell them the news and to see how they are going to act towards the situation.

"Mom, what's going on?" Chris asked.

"Come and sit down. I want to tell you guys something. I don't know how you will take this but mommy is having a baby." I said waiting to see what they were going to say.

"Cool, I hope I get a little brother so that we can beat up on Mya" Chris said running out of the room.

"Mommy, aren't we enough. You aint going to love me when the baby comes are you?" Mya said with tears running down her face my fiancé walked out of the room so that I could have talked to Mya.

"Look at me Mya. Mommy will always have time for you. You are my baby. My only girl, my princess. I will never not have time for my baby. No matter when the baby come mommy has enough love for you, the baby and your brother. Okay come here." I said holding my daughter. For the first time I just felt bad. I never heard Mya say that and for her to say that it really caught me off guard and I felt like I had to say the words that I knew was true. I would never put one child before the other it don't work like that in my world.

CHAPTER 16

What is the word struggle? It is something that I don't have to do anymore. I finally understand what life is like. I have 3 beautiful daughters that mean more to me than life itself. I have seen them hurt, I have felt their cries and I have seen them scared. But they know that mommy is always here. No matter what my daughters may have gone through in life and no matter how much hell they had to put up with to get here they are beautiful strong woman and mothers and I am proud of a 3 of my girls. They know that life is hard it comes with struggling, pains and suffering but the made it through and so could you.

ALICIA

What is the word struggle? It is something that I don't have to do anymore. I have to be a mother and a woman. I have been through a lot in my life with no father and getting pregnant at young age and on top getting raped and pregnant again but I would change my life because out of all my problems I gave birth to two beautiful little girls that have brighten my world. Kia and Zakiyah give me a reason to get up every day and keep it moving. They didn't ask to be brought into this world but they are here. And even though their fathers have putted them though so much pains they are still great kids. My babies still ended up with a better step-father that loves them with all his heart. Yes, I am married now and it feels good to have a man to help me and also to teach me how to learn to love again. A man I mean because I love my kids with my whole heart. Sometimes I don't know what I would do without my family. Understanding people is something that I am not trying to do anymore. I am trying to focus on my family and how I can make life better for us. I am blessed to be having another baby in the next 4 months. Yes, I am finally having my little boy. Zakiyah and Kia are so excited about the baby that they don't know what to do. I have learned a lot over my life and that is when you have struggled long enough God will open up the gates so that you won't have to hurt or struggle ever again. Believe it because it is true I am a live witness and so are you.

JASMINE

What is the word struggle? It is something that I don't have to do anymore. I love my life. I decided to take Chris, Mya and my fiancé to Kevin and Jamair grave today. I wanted my family to know that there was two other brothers and stepsons in the picture. My ex-husband stood crying over the graves. I still walked up so that way I could tell my kids that what they have been asking for has been in there faces the whole time. Their father. Without saying a word he turned around and hugged Mya and Chris. I think they remember who he was because a big smile had come over their faces. My fiancé knew that they had to find out so he just held me. I love this man he is the kind of man that I have prayed for. I am having another little boy in now 3 months and I am so excited. Understanding a man is something that I am not trying to do anymore. I have a good one. It gets to the point where you have struggled to try to make something work when God is really pulling it apart so that something better can take the place of something that you were supposed to lose. I learned to stop holding on to my past because it was messing up the future that God had for me. Sometimes ladies it is best to let go and let God. I did and now I got a family built around people that love me and is always going to be there. And I am engaged to a man that God has sent to me.

TIFFANY

What is the word struggle? It is something that I don't have to do anymore. Antonio passed away a couple of days ago. At the funeral I sat there and just thinking about the good days that we shared the laughs, the tears and our kids. I never knew how much I really loved this man until today. Even though we had a lot of hard days and a hell of a lot of good days. We ended up with 4 beautiful children and as I look at my babies I can see the hurt in their eyes. They miss their father so much. I know that I can't take his place in their hearts but I can be here for them the way that a mother should. I held all my babies in my arms and I told them that everything is going to be okay their father is always with them. He is in their heart and he is smiling down on each and every one of you. The love that Antonio had for his kids will never be forgotten. With understanding a man I found myself. I found out the kind of woman and mother it is that I am supposed to be. God has given me a chance to get to know what it is that I have to do for me and my kids. Sometimes we are so worried about what someone has done to us in the past that we don't know what we are doing to our selves at that point of time and I did. I learned to love life and to love myself and my kids and not worry about what was done to me yesterday. Even though the pain is still there I can't stop living. I got to go on for myself and my kids. And that what I am going to do.

CHAPTER 17

THE NEW BEGINNING

I know that you remember the 3 sisters: Tiffany Johnson, Alicia Smith-Jones, and Jasmine Smith-Williams. Well, they are back and now they are talking about their new beginning on how their has changed from last year until now.

TIFFANY

It's been a year since Antonio died. My kids are now understanding that daddy's gone. It was so hard at the funeral because they just don't understand why daddy died. They thought that daddy was coming back. For weeks I sat and watch my kids not play, not smile, just not doing anything I couldn't take it anymore so I sat them down and explain life and death to them.

"Listen, your daddy is in a better place and he wouldn't want you to stop having fun. Your daddy is watching you from heaven. He is smiling down on you. He is so proud of all of you. Baby, I know that it hurts but we can not put our lives on hold. Your father would not like that." I said. As the year ended I moved out the town even out of the state. I was offered job in South Carolina. Of course I had to rent a beautiful 3 bedroom house. I needed enough space for me and my 4 kids. South Carolina is so beautiful. It bothers me to be so far away from my mother and sisters but it's the best thing that I could have done for my kids and myself. The school is close to the house so it wouldn't be that far for me to walk the kids to school and walking each other back and forth home.

JASMINE

Last year was a good year I got married and gave birth to me to my now 6 month old baby boy D.J. which I named him after his father DeShawn Jr. Mya and Chris love their baby brother and they are such good help. After I gave birth to D.J. Chris would watch him while I slept for a little while. Mya helps me feed and change D.J. Shawn loves his baby boy. He stays home a lot now unless he got a game. My family is finally completed. I have a really good husband and 3 beautiful kids. What more can a woman ask for. My ex-husband comes by and picks up Mya and Chris every weekend. He is supposed to get them for a couple of months in the summer. We had to go to court for these orders but I feel that he is trying to change. I can't say that because I thought that he had changed the first time and I was wrong because I ended up loosing 2 of my kids. I visits Kevin and Jamair graves a lot. Just to say hi and to tell them how much I miss and love them. I still haven't fully got over it but I am working on it. Life is starting to look up.

ALICIA

Last year was a great year for me. I am finally married to my husband Dr. Joe Smith and we just gave birth to a beautiful baby boy which we named him Jay' Quan Smith. Jay for short. Being a mother for the 3rd time is beautiful I couldn't ask for anything different. Jay has just turned 8 weeks old today. He is such a happy, joyful little baby. Kia and Zakiyah love their little brother to death. I love it how my husband came in and took Kia and Zakiyah into his life and is raising them as if they were his. Since last year I have signed Kia up for theraphy. Everything that has happened in her life. I feel that it is important for her to get taught how to forgive her father for the wrong that he has put her though. I feel that the counseling is working because she is not as afraid as she was when it first happened. I am glad that she is much more understanding. I don't take her to see him and he keeps writing me asking me to bring her. I cant do that. I wont put my baby through that shit. I stay talking to my sister because we all have a great relationship and it means a lot to get help from them when I need them.

TIFFANY

My babies are starting their first day of school today. And I am so excited. I now understand what it means to survive. My job is going good. My mind seems to be on Antonio a lot lately. I dream about him touching me and kissing me again. I mean just making love to me again. I know that its been a year but I wish he was here with me. The kids don't really see me crying but I try to get over him but I cant. I miss him so much. You never know how much you love someone until they are gone. And that is a true statement. I woke up early this morning to fix my kids some breakfast. I had yet another dream about Antonio today. I just don't know what that means.

"Mommy, I cant get into the bathroom." A.J screamed.

"Okay, Nia come on out of the bathroom." I said. See this is what I got to go through in the morning time. As my kids get their selves together. I think that it is time for me to start dating again. I think that I am lonely. I know that I am don't know what to do. Can someone help me? I just am lost maybe to talk to adult about this.

"Hey ma. I need to talk to you about something important." I said packing the kids lunch.

"What's wrong Tiffany?" she said.

"I have been having dreams about Antonio lately. I just don't know what to do." I said.

"Baby girl you know that means that you are not over him." She said. But I already know that.

JASMINE

Today I am taking Mya and Chris to their father's house. I never seen my kids so excited to be going and see their father. My little man was sleeping so I got dressed AND HEADED OVER TO MY EX-HUSBAND'S HOUSE. My ex-husband is surprised that I am over here. I know that he still have feelings for me but I am past that level. I pulled up to his house as he stood outside with his girlfriend. Damn, she looks like a monster.

"Daddy!" the kids said jumping out of the car.

"Jasmine." He said coming to my passenger side window.

"I want my kids back the same way they were brought to you." I said.

"I got my kids." He said. Yeah that is the problem. I wanted to say something but I just didn't go there. I told my kids that I loved them and headed back to the house. 2 months without my kids. I don't know if I can handle that.

ALICIA

I received another letter from Kia's father today. He is still asking to see Kia and I am not having it. I really don't like having to keep Kia from her father. I know that it hurts Kia when she sees her brother and sister playing with their fathers. I hate seeing my little girl hurt but I got to protect her from him.

"Mommy, can I talk to you?" she asked as I changed Jay's diaper.

"Sure baby what's going on?" I said.

"Can I go and see my dad?" she asked.

"No Kia. We talked about this before. You're not ready baby." I said.

"Why not mommy?" she asked.

"I said no Kia. Now drop it." I said as she got up and stormed off. I hate telling her no but she got to understand I am doing what I feel is right. Her father is not a good guy and I'll be damned if I let him hurt her again. Seeing Kia upset really hurts me but I got to stand to my word about her going to see her dad. I am not trying to be mean. I just can't let her see her father right now. I tried talking to my husband about it and he really said things differently.

"Alicia, she is going to therapy. It might be good for her to go and talk to her father and tell him how she feels." He said.

"No it's not good right now. Honey, he has not only bruised once but twice. I just can't let my daughter keep going through this shit time after time again. What kind of mother would I be if I keep allowing him to do that." I said rocking Jay in my arms.

"I know but Alicia I still think that it would be a good idea." He said kissing me on my fore head.

"I don't think so. I don't want my child going to see him." I said. I cant say that I don't understand where he is coming from but he got to understand that I knows what is best for my daughter.

TIFFANY

My life without Antonio and raising my 4 kids is a struggle. It's really hard knowing that my kids are struggling knowing that their dad is not coming back. I have tried everyday to keep my kids happy. My mother was right for telling me that I am not over Antonio. But I don't know what to do. It's like I've tried to do everything but nothing seems to work. I think that I need help. Professional help. I decided to call my sister Jasmine. I know that she could help me out right now.

"Hey Tiff, what's going on?" she asked answering the phone.

"Jaz, I have been having dreams about Antonio. I don't know what to do." I said as I heard my nephew in the background.

"Sis, you can't expect your feelings to just fade away. He did just died last year. You got to focus on making a life for yourself and my nieces and nephews." She said. Damn, that is right. I can't put my life on hold. I know that I still love him. I really do but I wish that I could have made it work with him. But I cant dwell on it. I know what I got to do for me and that is what I am going to do.

JASMINE

I'm worried about my sister she is struggling so hard to get over Antonio. She is not over him. It's crazy how you can love a man that has done you so wrong and you don't know what to do. It's been two days and I am missing my kids like crazy.

"Mommy, I need to talk to you." Chris said.

"What's wrong baby?" I said feeding DJ

"I was wondering if I can stay with daddy." He said.

"Excuse me. What are you talking aout sweetie?" I said not understanding why my son want to leave me.

"I want to move with my dad." He said as I heard my ex-husband mouth in the background.

"Let me talk to your father." I said. I know that he is not putting anything bad in my son head about him leaving me.

"What Jasmine?" he said

"What the hell are you trying to do? Why are you trying to take my baby?" I asked upset and anger.

"I want my kids. And I will get them." He said hanging up. What the hell is going on? Why does he want to take my kids? Chris is not even his son and he want to take my kids. I swear if it's not one thing it's another. Every time I does the right thing. Something always goes wrong.

ALICIA

I never saw Kia as mad as she is right now. She knows that I love her and I am trying to do what I got to do to protect her. I took her to her counselor today to see what the hell can I do I don't want my daughter to be hurt. Am I wrong? I sat outside with Zakiyah and Jay in the waiting room. While Kia talked to her therapist. Kia came out of the room with a smile on her face. She ran into my lap and hugged me.

For the first time I know that she knows that I am trying to do what I feel is right to protect my daughter.

"Mrs. Smith, may I speak to you for a moment" her therapist said.

"Yes ma. Sit here for a minute babies. Mommy will be right back." I said walking into the room.

"Mrs. Smith, I talked to Kia and she was explaining to me how she wanted to go and see her father. I understand that she went through a traumatic situation and I feel that it would be a good idea for her to go and see her father." She said.

"No ma. I understand how you feel but my daughter is not going to see her father. He has done wrong things to her. I don't want my daughter hurt again." I said.

"Mrs. Smith, I understand I do but it's not going to make her feel better until she goes and see him. She is really handling her issue very well. I know that she has the understanding that she needs to make it through." She said. But I still didn't agree with her. I feel that my daughter still should not go and she her father.

"Thank you for being concern but I know how to handle my daughter." I said grabbing Jay and heading out of the door. Later at home I sat Kia down. Maybe I am being to hard on her. She is 7 years old and I feel that she is at the age that if anything happens she knows how to come to me and tell me about it.

"Kia, I made a decision. It seems that you really want to see your father and I think it is time for you to go up and see him." I said.

"Thank you mommy." She said jumping into my arms. I hope that I am doing the right thing.

TIFFANY

"Hi, I am looking to see a doctor." A man said walking up to me.

"Yes sir, I need for you to fill out these papers." I said handing him the papers.

"Thank you." He said filling out the papers. It felt good to be back at work. Just to clear my head of all the things that I have been thinking about. I never imagined being so lonely. I have tried everything.

"Hi again." The man said.

"Hi." I said looking at him.

"Why do you look so sad?" he asked taking a seating in front of me.

"It's nothing but how can I help you?" I said.

"I was just wondering why a beautiful woman is looking down." He said. Damn, he is really trying to get at me.

"Thank you for the compliment but I got to get to work." I said as a lady walked in with a little girl that seemed to be sick. After work I went and picked up my children from school. It was like I saw the light. I never had someone to come to me with a compliment before. It really makes me feel good. It feels really good for someone to tell me how good I look.

JASMINE

Today I received a letter in the mall saying that my ex-husband is trying to fight for full custody of Mya and Chris. Are you fucking kidding me? Every time I try to be nice to this ass he goes and does something fucking stupid. What I look like giving him my kids?

"What the hell are you trying to do? Why will you take my kids from me?" I said talking to him on the phone.

"My kids need to be with their father." He said.

"ARE YOU SERIOUS? Chris and Mya are fine where they are. You are lucky that you got any chance to see them at all. Must I remind you that you were the cause odf my babies getting killed." I said pissed off now.

"Why do you have to keep going there? You think that it don't hurt me to know that my kids are dead. They were not only your kids Jaz. Why we are on this. Do you know how it feels to have a ex wife that you still love married to someone else and had his baby? Did you even think about how that feels Jasmine?" he said hanging up. I looked at D.J. I love the life that I live right now. I have a wonderful husband and 3 kids. What more can I ask for?

CHAPTER 18

ALICIA

Today is the day that Kia goes and visit her father. I am still upset about letting her but if everyone says that its alright I will go along with it.

"Honey, are you sure that you have Jay and Zakiyah until I get back?" I said as I handed Jay to his daddy.

"Yes baby, I got them. Now go ahead and take Kia to see her father." He said. I pulled up to the jailhouse with Kia. I could tell that she was very nervous but she wouldn't tell me.

"Mommy." She said.

"Yes baby." I said.

"I scared Mommy." She said.

"Mommy, will be there with you. I am not going to let anything happen to you." I said grabbing her hand. As we walked into the jailhouse and the doors slammed behind us. Kia jumped.

"It's okay baby. Mommy got you." I said. We walked in and her father was sitting at the table with a big smile on his face. He acted as if he hasn't seen his daughter in years. I know that it has been a year but damn. As we walked up Kia hide behind me.

"Hi Kia." He said standing up to hug her but she wouldn't go to him.

"Everyone have a seat." He said.

"Daddy, I am glad that mommy had let me come and see you." Kia said.

"Happy late birthday Kia. Thank you Alicia for bringing my daughter to come and see me." He said. I still don't have too many words to say to him. I watch as Kia and her father talked and laughed. But not once did he say that he was sorry for what he had did to her. He can tell her happy birthday but he can't say sorry to her.

"Alicia, is it okay for me to have a minute alone with Kia." He said.

"You know that is not going to happen." I said. What the hell is wrong with him asking me something like that. He must be crazy.

"Daddy, I got a little brother now. Mommy is married and she had a baby." Kia said.

"What? Alicia I know that you don't have another man around my daughter." He said getting angry.

"I sure do. She needs a father because you aint one. Kia give your father a hug so we can leave." I said. He must think I care about how he feels but I don't because my daughter is being taken care of and that is all that matters.

TIFFANY

I feel so alone down here. Its like I have no one in my corner to tell me what to do. I cant get over him. The more that I try the harder it is for me o move on. I don't want to move from here because it is a chance for me to finally do something for Tiffany. It time for Tiffany to make a life for her and her kids. I love Antonio indeed I do but I just cant see myself keep crying over him anymore. Everyone is telling me that I aint over him. And maybe it is true. But what do you do? You gave a man your whole life with 4 beautiful kids and he leaves you. He dies and you are alone. How can you leave me alone twice? I am so mad at him. Everything in me hates him.

"I hate you Antonio." I said falling on the floor in tears. Nia walked into the room and ran into my arms.

"Mommy, its okay." She said. I cant keep doing this. From here on out I got to move on. I cant continue to keep crying and allowing my kids to see me like this but it hurts so much.

JASMINE

My wonderful husband came home today.

"Hey honey." He said kissing me on the lips.

"Hey babe." I said laying D.J down for a nap.

"Why you sound so down?" he asked grabbing a cold beer out of the frig.

"My ex-husband is taking me to court to get custody of Chris and Mya." I said trying not to break down into tears.

"Babe, we got this. Don't worry we are not going to loose them." He said.

"How do you know that Shawn? I can't loose my kids." I said upset. I know that I shouldn't get mad at Shawn. But he don't know what can happen. The judge can g rant him custody and he can take my babies. Chris nor Mya called me today. It hasn't even been a week yet and I just don't know what to do with myself. I cant eat, I can barely sleep because all I can think about is me loosing my kids. What is a woman to do?

ALICIA

I have seen a change in Kia since she went to see her father. Even though he hasn't apologize for what he has done to her but she was still so happy. She smiled all the way home. I know Kia's father is very upset that another man was being the father in her life. But I don't have a choose but to do what's right for my baby.

"Mommy, thank you for taking me to see my daddy." Kia said.

"Your welcome baby." I said. I am glad to see Kia so happy. Zakiyah's father decided to come and see her today. I can't stand this man sometimes. He wants to be a father when he feels like it.

"Where's my baby?" he said

"Playing with her daddy." I said.

"Don't start that stupid shit Alicia. You know that he is not her dad. I am." He said.

"Well, if you act like a father maybe your daughter might know you." I said pissed off.

"I am busy Alicia. I make time when I can to see Zakiyah. Now can I see her." He said heading to the door. I just let him leave. I don't know why he is the way that he is. After all that he has done to me. He wants to now step up and be a father to his daughter after he didn't want anything to do with her. I won't let my kids hurt anymore. That's what a real mother does, and baby I am a real mother.

TIFFANY

After having my break down. I really felt less of a mother. I decided to move back home. I packed up and left everything in South Carolina; my house, my job shit everything. I have to go back home. I need my family. I cant get this without them. I know that my mother would let me stay with her so when I came into town and we went to her house.

"Mom." I called knocking on the door.

"Tiffany, come in baby. What are you doing here?" she is opening the door.

"I want to come back home mom. Can me and the kids stay with you?" I said.

"You know that you can." My mom said. I know that my mom is always there.

DESHAWN

My daughters are going through something again Tiffany is moving back in with me. I know that its only been a year since Antonio died but she gots to get over it. My granddaughter called me and told me she was crying over him. I don't know what to do about my daughter. She is loosing her mind. I got to get my daughter back together. She is crazy to be going crazy over this man. Jasmine and Alicia is trying to do good things in life but I got to keep a eye on them too. I guess the older that your kids get the more that you got to keep a eye on them.

JASMINE

Shawn is still mad at me. I didn't mean to get mad at him but he don't know how it feels to loose your kids. My ex-husband was nice enough to let me come and see my kids. I know that he only got them for 2 months but I need to see them just to make sure they are okay. I left DJ at home with his daddy.

"Mommy." Mya yelled as I got out of the car.

"Hey baby girl." I said picking her up. I held my daughter tight in my arms. I love to see them smile.

"Jasmine, I need to talk to you." My ex-husband said.

"Theres nothing that we need to talk about. I just want to spend time with my kids." I said watching Mya play. Chris really didn't say to much to me but its okay because he can not move in with his dad.

ALICIA

Zakiyah cried half the night because her father didn't have time to spend with her. It hurts me to know that he don't want to spend anytime. It just don't make any sense to keep hurting her. I am a good mother but there is only so much that I can do. Maybe its time to cut him out her life all together. I don't want to do that but what choose do I have. I need to talk to my mom. I got my babies dressed and headed over to my mother's house.

"Tiffany, what are you doing back." I said hugging her with Jay in my arms.

"I come back to be with my family. South Carolina was to far away and I missed you guys." She said grabbing Jay.

"I am glad your back where's mom." I said Kia and Zakiyah went into the living room.

"Hey baby girl." My mom said hugging me tight.

"Mom, John came by and he just don't want to be bothered with Zakiyah." I said sitting at the table.

"Don't worry about him. You got a husband and three beautiful kids focus on that and leave the asshole alone. If he don't want t take care of his responsibility you got another man that will." She said. My mother is right I got a good husband at home that love my kids. I know that its John's lost not mine.

CHAPTER 19

DESHAWN

If it aint one thing its another. John don't want to take care of responsibilities as a father. I swear the men that my daughters get involved with. I taught my daughters to never count on a man because all they will do is leave you high and dry and that is a true statement. All the men in my girls life has done something wrong. I am just waiting for these men too.

TIFFANY

Being back home again is a beautiful feeling. I felt so alone in South Carolina. My sisters are coming by too see me today. As I laid in my bed. I saw a small brown box at the foot of my bed.

"Good morning Tif." My mom said standing in the doorway.

"Good morning mom. Do you know where this box came from?" I said sitting up.

"Yes. Antonio came to the house before he died and he told me to give this to you and before I could you left." She said. Why is Antonio leaving stuff for me? I hope it can explain to me why he left me with 4 kids. Jasmine and Alicia came by. I havent seen Jay since he was born and now I can.

"Alicia, he is so cute? How old is he?" I said holding my nephew.

"He's 8 weeks old." She said taking Zakiyah's coat off. It felt good to see my sister and my nieces and nephews. I wondered why Mya and Chris isn't here.

"Jaz, where's Chris and Mya?" I said kissing Jay.

"With their daddy for the summer." She said playing with D.J. I know that a lot of things is wondering in my mind about my nieces and nephews being over there at their fathers house. I don't even like the idea of them being over there with him. But what can I say.

JASMINE

It feels so good to have Tiffany back home. Its been 5 months since I saw my sister and the kids. Everyday my nieces and nephews are getting so big. I can see it in her eyes that she aint over Antonio. Its crazy because he did her wrong just like my ex-husband did to me. Don't get me wrong I love my ex-husband I really do but he has changed. I remember when I was pregnant with Chris and I met him he was the perfect most sexiest man that I have ever seen. He was 5'9, dark skinned with a nice faded cut. He was just a man that was not scared to go after what he wanted. From that moment on I knew that I had found the man that I wanted to be with forever. But I tell you people do change.

Don't get me wrong I love Shawn. I really do but my heart still belongs to my ex-husband. I just cant be with him. What am I saying? I got a good husband. I don't know I am so confused.

ALICIA

It's a good thing that I have a supportive family. I am glad that my big sister is back home. I thought about John all night and how he hurted by baby but I cant be mad at him I am mad at myself for trying to give him a chance to be a father to his daughter but he turns around and does this. I will not and I do mean will not punish my kids not for something their stupid father's did. As I played with my nieces I saw the new channel come on Shawn has escaped from jail. Oh damn, I wonder what's going to happen now. I got to watch my kids very closely now. I cant believe that this nigga is out on the run. Man, I hope he don't start anything stupid. What can a mother do? Everyday it is something.

"Honey, what is wrong?" Joe said as he walked into the living room with Jay in his arms.

"Shawn, escaped my jail and I know that he is coming after Kia." I said as I grabbed Jay.

"Honey, you don't have to worry about anything. It is not going to happen like that. Don't worry baby." Joe said. But he don't know how Shawn is. I know this man and I know what he is capable of. I am so worried about my babies now.

TIFFANY

After my sisters left and I put my kids to bed. I opened the box that had a lot of letters in it.

February 14

Dear Tiffany,

I am writing to tell you Happy Valentines Day. I know that we are not together but every day since we broke up I've been thinking about you. I want you to know that I love you more than anyone I've ever knew. Its something in your eyes that made me fell in love with you. All those girls that said something about our relationship wanted what we had. The past 9 years that we've been together has been the best time of my life. Thank you for giving me 4 beautiful children. I love you Tiffany. I know that I did you wrong and I know that I hurt you. But baby I love and I want you to know that I will never put another person in front of you. I know that you can't forgive me for everything that I have done to you. I still do want you to marry me? I love you Tiffany.

Love yours truly,

Antonio

After reading this letter it brought tears to my eyes. All of the beating that I used to get from Antonio it doesn't matter anymore as long as I had him in my life. I know I sound stupid but love makes you say some stupid shit. I miss him so much.

JASMINE

Today I received a call from my ex-husband asking me to come quick to his house. D.J. and Shawn was sleeping so I sneaked out the house.

"What's wrong?" I said as I pulled into the driveway.

"Nothing. I need to talk to you." He said as I got out of the car.

"About what? There's nothing that we need to talk about." I said.

"I'm sorry Jaz. I am sorry about everything I did. The death of our boys. Signing the divorce papers baby I still love you. Jasmine, I love you." He said.

"Now, you love me. Now that I've done moved on you love me." I said as tears rolled down my face.

"I did you wrong. I never helped with the kids, I cheated on you. I am sorry." He said kissing me. The kiss became powerful. I couldn't believe what my hands was doing. I started unbuttoning his shirt. And he took off my clothes and we headed to the bedroom. As we went around and around. I felt alive wait! What the hell am I doing? I'm married. Oh my goodness!

"I have to go this was a mistake." I said throwing my clothes on and headed home.

ALICIA

I can't believe that he has escaped from jail. Shawn is crazy.

"Alicia." He whispered as I came to my car.

"What are you doing Shawn?" I said.

"I want to see Kia" he said.

"Get out of here. Shawn you will not see her now get lost." I said.

"I will get to see my daughter." He said. I can't believe that he came here and he is asking to see Kia. I can't tell anyone that I saw him. I still don't know what I'm going to do. As I left my mother's house I noticed that John had passed by. I feel that they got something planned and I hope my daughters don't have anything to do with it. They want to try to hurt me and they know what would hurt me if they messed with my girls. I just don't know what to do with these girls. I try to help them out by letting them see their kids and now I see that I got to go through this shit.

TIFFANY

Dear Tiffany,

I have a secret to tell you that I have hiding from you. I cheated on you when we were together. I am sorry Tiffany. The time that you gave birth to the twins I cheated. I am truly sorry baby. I love you.

Love you always,

Antonio

I knew he cheated on me but I never wanted to believe it. Now he wants to write letters confessing everything that he had did. I decided to stop reading the letters confessing everything that he had did. It's crazy because it took me back to how it was when we was together and when he was alive. I cant live my life is like this anymore. I gots to move on. I keep telling myself that I am going to move but I cant I don't have the strength too.

JASMINE

I pulled up home and just sat in my car. I cant believe that I slept with my ex-husband. Shawn is a good man and a great father how could I do this to him. What should I do he might leave me.

"Babe, where you at?" he said as I answered my phone.

"I am in the car." I said.

"Come inside so we could talk." He said. I . . . . I don't know what to do. I walked into the house my baby had dinner made with candles.

"Where's D.J?" I ask taking off my coat.

"I layed him down for a nap. I decided that you work so hard and I just want to show you that I appreciate you . . ." He said pulling out a chair. I started t cry.

"Baby, what wrong?" he asked as tears rolled down my face.

"Nothing, I am just so lucky to have you." I said as he wiped the tears from my face. I just don't know what I am going to do.

ALICIA

I put my babies to bed and waited for my husband to come home from work. I am worried more now that Shawn is out. I know I should report him but I don't want Kia to find out that he father is out. As I sat waiting I heard Jay start to cry. I know what this mean its feeding time.

"Hold on baby. Mommy's coming." I said walking in his room. I picked up my sons and headed into the kitchen and heated him up a bottle. I feed the baby as my husband walked into the house.

"Hey honey." I said as I continued to feed Jay.

"Baby, let me go and see my girls." He said kissing me and walking into the girls room. He hurried up and came back out.

"Alicia, where's the girls?" he said

"They are in the bed." I said trying to burp Jay.

133

"Honey, they are not in their room." He said.

"What the hell are you talking about? I just put them to bed about a hour ago." I said getting up. When I walked into their room my daughters was not there. Oh hell, no he took my babies. I KNOW IT! I KNEW IT.

"Honey please call the cops. He done took my kids." I said as I laid Jay down in his crib. I can't believe that again he would hurt me. Why me? Why do he keep doing this to me? My girls. My daughters. Who knows what he would do to them now? I cant believe this. I cant even keep myself calm I just want to hurt him right now. My babies.

TIFFANY

I decided to get up this morning and took my kids to the park until I noticed that my mother was up and very pissed off.

"What's wrong mom?" I said sitting down beside her.

"I just got off the phone with Alicia trying to calm her down." My mom started

"What's going on mom?" I said worried.

"Zakiyah and Kia is missing. And to top it off Shawn escaped from jail. I just don't know. That man keeps trying to hurt my baby and I just cant understand why." My mother said as tears rolled down her face. I just knew that man was going to do something to my sister. She is trying to maintain a new life, with a new man and her 3 kids but her baby's fathers makes it so hard for her to do anything right and that is so wrong. I just cant believe this. I went back into the back and got the kids ready and we headed over to my sisters house. When we got there the police was asking Joe a lot of questions and Alicia was in the back room crying. It hurted me to see my sister like this. I hate that my little sister is struggling like this. All the problems that I am going through with Antonio death my sister has been here for me and I am going to be there for her.

"Hi." One of the officers said.

"Hi." I said.

"I want you to know we are doing everything to find them." He said. It's crazy I can't believe that this is happening again. How much more does she need to go through. My sister is a good person. All she does is try to do right by these guys and they treats her like this. I know how a man can have kids and do them and their mothers the way that Shawn and John is doing my sister. It is crazy. I tried comforting my sister but it gets so hard. She is real fighting to handle this situation. I just don't know what to do. I hope she can pull through this.

JASMINE

As much drama that is going on in this family something got to give. My sister kids got kidnapped. I just can't believe this shit. I got D.J dressed and hurried up over to my sister's house. My sister is crying and all broken up. This man has put my sister through so much stuff. It's a blessing that she is still strong. I am standing by my sister holding her up but its so hard I don't know . . . Wait I do know how it is too loose your kids. Its crazy she got to go through this. I just don't understand why some people just can't understand that it is wrong to hurt a woman. And I mean a woman by taking away their kids. It was a very hurtful feeling. It is something that you can't get rid of. It is a bad feeling when you can't hold your kids. You can't kiss your babies and you can't do anything with your kids. I know the pain that my sister is feeling. But I just don't know how someone can take kids man. What kind of person does that? What kind of man hurt is baby mother? A good one at that. It is just so crazy how men are no a days.

ALICIA

I am going crazy. I miss my daughters. My mother, my husband and my sisters are here and they are trying to calm me down. I am worried about my girls.

"Ma, I'm take this report in but we cant do anything yet because they haven't been missing for 24 hours." The officer said.

"Sir, my 6 and 7 year old daughters are missing and that all your going to do is take a damn report. I don't want to hear that I want him found and I want my daughters are home with me." I said. Jay was crying in my husbands arms so I took him and rocked him to sleep. I want my girls back. I still got to be a mom to my son as well. I got to hold it together. I know that they will be home to me soon. I just cant get it out of my mind that this man has taken my girls. I know that he wanted to see Kia but why take Zakiyah. She is not even his daughter. This just don't make any sense to me. Not at all.

CHAPTER 20

DESHAWN

I cant stand this shit. This man done come and taken my granddaughters. What the hell is wrong with him. My daughter has been through a lot with Shawn now he done broken out of jail and kidnapped my granddaughter's. Alicia is flipping out. She don't know what to do. She needs mommy and mommy is here. After everyone left and thing calmed down I had laid my grandson down and walked back into the room where my daughter was but she was still crying and flipping out.

"Alicia, baby girl are you okay?" I said as I sat on the bed beside her.

"No mom, I just don't know what to do? I miss my girls. Why does he keep doing this to me? Mom all I did was do what I think was right by keeping my kids away from him. I thought that was the right thing to do for my daughter. But look what has happened?" she said as she started crying again.

"Alicia, baby it is okay. You did everything that you was supposed to do. Don't you start feeling bad you did what you was supposed to do because you did sweetie. You did." I said as I held her. I just can't believe that this is happening again. Just seeing my daughter like that made my mind go wild but I know that I had to hold it together for her.

TIFFANY

Watching my sister hurt this way is very painful. The police officers and my sister was going back and forth through the house as my mother held the baby. I headed home to put the kids to bed. I know that my sister was going through a lot and I wish that there was something more that I could do to change it. As I tucked my kids into the bed. I sat up waiting for my mom to come home. I am so worried about my sister.

"Mom, how is Alicia?" I said as she walked in the door.

"Barely, holding it together. She is trying to be strong but it so hard." She said sitting down. I know that this just didn't make any sense. How could he keep hurting my little sister like this. Everything that she has done for these no good men. They don't how hard it is to be a single mother. It is no joke. It is no joke to be fighting to take care of your kids all by their selves. Having to get them up in the morning, getting them dress, then you got to feed them, and wash their clothes and everything else. It is so hard.

JASMINE

I don't know what to do. First, I cheated on my husband and now my nieces was kidnapped. This is just so crazy. After spending a few hours I went home to my husband.

"Hey baby. Hand me the baby. I will put him to sleep while you go get in the hot water tub that I made for you." He said taking D.J out of my arms. Damn, what am I going to do? I love my husband I really do. But how can I sleep with my ex-husband. After my husband placed D.J down he came into the bathroom and got in the tub with me. He started messaging my back and kissing me on the neck and turned me around and started kissing me on the lips. Damn, his lips was so soft. And he went in me. No, this is wrong I shouldn't be having sex in this tub right now but it feels so damn good. As he pushed in deeper and held my legs tighter I knew he wanted it. He carried me out of the tub to the bed where he just keeping going deeper and deeper. He was making me scream for him like I never did. But then I made the biggest mistake of my life. I screamed out my ex-husbands name. Damn, I am fucked now.

"WHAT THE HELL?" my husband said as he pushed me off the top of him.

"Baby, I am sorry." I said but I knew that it was to damn late.

"Jasmine, are you serious? You are laying here making love to me and calling out another mans name. What the hell is going on?." He said getting up and putting his clothes on and walking out of the door. I know that I have pissed him off. I cant believe this shit I cant believe that came out of my mouth. I cant believe that I had said that. What am I thinking I don't want to loose my husband. I don't want to mess up the good thing that we have right now. I sat on my bed me and waited for my husband to come back home. It is crazy. As I watched the time he still has not showed up yet. I tried calling him time after time after time again. I cant believe that he has not came home yet. Oh my goodness I hope he comes home to me.

ALICIA

My husband is so supportive right now. I couldn't ask for a better man than him.

"Honey, I am supposed to go to work today but I will stay home if you need me too." He said as we sat down on the couch.

"No baby go to work and if I hear something I will call you." I said. I still cant believe that this man took my kids. Looking into Jay's eyes helps me hold it together. I know that I cant flip because my babies needing me. My daughters maybe scared and alone right now. A knock came to my door it was John. Damn this is the last thing that I need.

"What do you want?" I said holding Jay angry and pissed.

"Look, I am sorry." He said

"Where is my daughters? I don't know. What are you saying Zakiyah is gone." He said acting like a damn fool.

"What do you mean that she's gone?" he said.

"She's not here." I said as he sat down. I cant believe that he don't know where she's at. What am I to do? I know that Shawn took my girls and I want them home with me right now. I know that John wants to help me but I just don't think that it is the right time for all of this. John sat on the couch and was trying to call up everyone to see if anyone have seen the girls but to my surprise no one has. I sat on the couch and held Jay in my arms and rocking him back and forth. Man, he looks just like my girls. He has their smiles, lips and everything. But the only different is that he is a shade darker then my girls. I have noticed that ever since the girls been gone. Jay has not been acting the same. He has been crying and everything. He is so use to the girls coming into the room and playing with him. With them not here it is very hard. I just don't know what to do. Everyone is trying to keep there head up for me but it is so hard for me to keep my head together. I am really trying to hold my head up and keep it together because I know that my girls are so scared and afraid right now. I just got to keep my focus on trying to bring my babies home to me.

TIFFANY

It feels so good being in my own bed again. I am just trying to start a new leaf. My sister is trying to keep herself together and I know that it is hard. I really got to be here for her. It has been a week and I am not having to many dreams about Antonio but my babies still be crying and calling out his name. I don't even know how to began to help them.

"Mommy, can I talk to you?" Ja'Nia said walking into my room.

"Yes baby. Come on in." I said as she came and laid on my lap.

"Mommy, I miss my daddy. I wish he was here right now. Mommy, why did daddy have to die. Why he had to leave us." Ja'Nia said as she cried.

"Ja'Nia I know baby. It hurts but I am here and I am going to take care of you. I miss your father too baby. But it is going to be okay. You hear me baby girl it is going to be okay." I said as I held her in my arms. I know that it hurts my kids not to have there father in their lives but I am trying so hard be there for their for them and still deal with the lost of Antonio. Tomorrow is the day that me and Antonio first got together. It was our first date. Damn, I miss him so much. I just know that I got to pull myself together for my kids and show them that we are going to be okay. I know that we will be okay.

JASMINE

Its crazy that my husband was so upset that he went to go and visit his mother and he took our son with him. Sitting at home I am so confused. A knock came to my door.

"Hey Jaz." My ex husband said as I looked with total shock.

"What are you doing here?" I said as I tried to close the door but he pinned me against the wall and started kissing me.

"Stop! . . . ." I started but instead I headed up to my bed room as he followed up the steps. We got to the room and he laid me down on the bed. He started kissing me and taking my clothes off. My phone must had rung a hundred times but it felt so damn good. What am I saying this is wrong?

"Jaz, I miss you. I want you back. I want our family back together." He said as he kissed me on the forehead.

"I cant you know I am married now. I cant just leave my husband like that. He is a real good man Eric. He is a great father to my kids. I just can't do it." I said sitting up.

"Jasmine, so why keep sleeping with me. Cant no other man touch you the way that I can not even your own husband." Eric said getting dressed.

"You got to go." I said pushing him down the stairs and out of the door. I cant believe that I just did that. Oh my god! What am I going to do. I love my life. How could I be so stupid? He wants me to leave my family and come back to him. I don't think so. I cant do that to my husband he is such a good man. I love Deshawn so much. I cant believe that I am hurting him the way that I am.

ALICIA

I still sit here thinking about the fact that my girls are gone. What does he want from me? What more can I do that I haven't already done. He seen Kia and he shot her, then I still let him see her and then he rapes her and I thought that I was doing the right thing. Now look my girls are gone. I really just don't know what else to do. I don't know how I put myself in this position. As I pick up my son and feed him the thought about what could happen to my girls I just don't know what to do. My husband came home and I was laying on the couch with my baby sleeping in my arms.

"Honey have you heard anything about our girls." He said kissing me on the lips and kissing the baby on the head.

"Hell no. I wish my that someone would tell something." I said as I gently tap my son's back.

"Honey, you got to calm down okay. Our girls will come home to us." He said.

"When? You don't know my baby father like I do. I just want them home and in my arms that's all." I said. I know that my husband is trying to help but I just don't know right now. I don't know what I am going to do.

TIFFANY

Today! Today! Today! It was the first date that me and Antonio went on. He came to my house with flowers and a candy. He looked so sharp and he took me to a fancy restaurant. I mean he went all out. He was starring at me with a light shining in his eyes. Then he asked me to dance. Of course I said yes. But the way that he grab my hip and we slow dance. It must had been something about that night that made me want to be with Antonio. But it was something because I had 4 babies by him. Sometimes it hurts being single parent but I hold it together for my kids.

"Mommy, are you okay." Nia said.

"Yes baby, I am fine. Go do your homework." I said.

"Yes ma." She said heading out the room. I cooked dinner and I got the table set so the kids could eat. Lord, please give me the strength to move on. Please Lord help me to move on. I prayed. I know the Lord will hear my pray and help me. I can't do this all alone.

JASMINE

My husband and D.J returned today. But I don't know if I should let him know or keep it to myself. I don't want to lie to my husband. But I don't want to leave me with 3 kids. I am so confused. He still isn't talking to me but I got to be honest and tell him.

"Honey, may I talk to you?" I asked as I walked into the room.

"What Jasmine?" he said sitting on the bed.

"Honey, I need to talk to you." I said.

"What's wrong?" He said putting the bags down and laying D.J in his crib.

"Baby, I love you with all my heart but I have been cheating on you with my ex-husband." I said as his faced turned to a angry face. He say a word he just walked out the door. Damn, I don't what to loose my family. I don't want to loose my husband. I sat down and cried on the couch wondering how could I let my ex-husband touch me knowing I love my husband.

SHAWN

I cant believe what came out of my wife's mouth. How could she cheat on me. We have a family together. We got a 6 month old son. I love this woman and our kids. But I just don't know what to do. This has my mind all messed up. I am in a place that I don't know if I can come back from. I don't know what to do. This is a hard situation. I just don't know what to do.

CHAPTER 21

ALICIA

I sat up all night. I just don't know where to start at. This man just wont give me my girls back.

"Honey, you need to get some sleep." Joe said as a knock came to the door.

"I cant sleep can you get that while I feed the baby." I said getting a bottle out of the frig and heating it up.

"Mr. Smith, we got some good news and some bad news." The police officer said.

"What's the news officer." Joe said.

"We found your kids. But Shawn was killed. He had a gun and we had to take them down." He said.

"HONEY!" Joe screamed.

"Whats wrong?" I said as I ran into the living room feeding the baby.

"They found our girls but Shawn was killed." Joe said.

"Sir, where are my girls?" I said as tears rolled down my face.

"Hold on let me go and get them." He said as I handed Jay to his father and I followed behind the police officer.

"Come on girls. Someone wants to see you." He said.

"MOMMY!" they said running into my arms tears rolled down my face as I held the girls tight. I didn't even want to let them go. John walked up.

"Zakiyah." He said but she wouldn't go to him. She ran to Joe and Kia continued to hold me tight.

"Kia. Baby mommy got you. I will never let this happen again. Go in the house I am coming." I said as she ran to Joe.

"Alicia, what do I do? My daughter wont even come to me or anything." He said sitting on my steps.

"John, just leave her alone. When she's ready she will let you know. You and your brother have hurted my babies for the last time." I said as I walked into the house. I am glad my girls are home at last.

TIFFANY

I decided to get out my sowers and try to do something. I got my kids dressed and decided to take them to the park. Something to get everything that I am dealing with off of my head. I watched as my kids laughed and played. To see them smile was the best feeling in the world. Just to understand I know that I got to do better for my kids.

"Hi. Is anyone sitting here." A fine man said.

"No, you can have a seat." I said.

"I have been looking at you for a while. My name is Xavier." He said.

"Hi Xavier. My name is Tiffany." I said with a smile on my face.

"Well, I know that I just met you but I would really like to take you and your kids out to dinner with me and my son tomorrow." He said. Wow, a man asked me out and he want to take my kids.

"How about this I cook and you and your son tomorrow at my house." I said.

"Okay. See you tomorrow Mrs. Tiffany." He said as he got up and walked off with his son. Wow, I think that I got a date with a man that's not Antonio. Well, I got to get my babies home before it gets to dark.

JASMINE

My husband hasn't talked to me since I told him that I slept with Mya and Chris father. We don't even sleep in the same bed. I am so scared I don't want to loose my family. I really don't want my husband to leave me.

"Deshawn, baby can we talk?" I said walking into the living room holding Jr.

"Jasmine, We have nothing to talk about. You know I just don't know if I can trust you. How could you do that to me. I never cheated on you with anyone. Why do that to me? Do you want to loose me and our baby? Do you want this family to be over?" he said grabbing DJ out of my hands.

"Honey, its not like that. I am sorry. Deshawn, I don't want to loose our family behind this. Baby I am sorry." I said crying. He just started playing with the baby and paying me no attention. Okay I deserve everything that he is doing but I don't know what to do. I don't want to loose my husband. I really love him. I made a mistake. Hell, a lot of woman do but at least I told him.

ALICIA

Its only been a couple of days since Kia and Zakiyah been home. I have seen a dramatic change in my girls. They don't even say anything about what has happened to them. I don't know what the hell to do.

"Hi, girls. What are you doing?" I said walking into their room. They looked at me and said nothing. I just don't know what to do. They just looked out the window and didn't say anything. I don't even like this at all.

"Honey have they said anything yet?" My husband said as he changed the babies diapers.

"Nope nothing. And I am worried about that. I really think that we need to get them some counseling again." I said as I sat on the bed.

"Babe are you sir that is good idea? Maybe we need to wait and see if they come around and tell us themselves." He said cleaning up Jay and putting a clean outfit on him. I just don't understand what I am supposed to do. I don't like to see my kids down like this. I just don't know what to do to help them. I cant believe this shit. My girls wont come out their room for anything. I swear that I need to find a away to help my girls. It is so hard to sit and look at them like this. I need to go and talk to my mo just to get some advice.

"Hey mom." I said walking into the house.

"Where's the kids?" my mom said hugging me.

"With Joe but I came because I don't know what to do about my girls. Ever since the came home they have not been the same and I am scared. I don't know how to help them. I have tried talking to them and nothing seems to work what do I do mom." I said sitting down and pouring a glass of juice.

"Baby girl, I understand that you want to help the girls but sweetie you got to let them come to you and just be patient. They will come around they are scared baby that's all." My mom and she is true. I think I am going to let my girls come to me and tell me what he did to them? I know that he did something. I just don't know what.

TIFFANY

Its crazy. Today is the day that Xavier and his son supposed coming to my house and having dinner with me and the kids.

"Babies, mommy needs you to come. And get yourself ready for tonight." I said preparing the meal. I just hope that my kids be on their best behavior. Time passed and my doorbell rung and it was Xavier and his little boy.

"Please come in." I said as my babies stood behind me.

"Hi." Xavier said handing me flowers.

"Thank you. These are my kids; Nia, A.J, Ja'Nia and Ja'Mair." I said.

"Nice to meet you all this is my son Malachi." He said. We sat down at table and began to have dinner it felt so good to have a man sitting at a dinner table. To. see my kids smile at another man that's not their daddy felt good. I love Antonio but it is time to move on. I can't continue to live like this. I want to be happy.

JASMINE

I don't know what to do right now. I am so confused. Shawn gets up just leave out the house. I sit home all day with D.J hoping and praying that me and my husband come back together as one. I think that I can at least hold my husband again.

"Honey, can we talk?" I said while D.J was napping.

"Jasmine, I sit here and just wondered what is it that you want. I am a good husband. A damn good husband and I just want to know what else do you want?" he said.

"Baby, I want you. I want our family. You is a good man and I love you babe." I said.

"Jaz, I just don't know. I don't know if I can forgive you right now." He said.

"Deshawn, I said sorry what more can I say?" I said but he just got up and headed out the door. I couldn't say anything. My ex-husband stopped by today to get Chris and Mya. Damn, the last thing I need is Deshawn seeing him.

"Jaz, is the kids ready." He said pissed off that I haven't got back to him.

"Yeah, let me go and get them." I said running upstairs to get them." I said running upstairs to get the kids ready.

"Mommy, I don't want to go." Mya said sitting on the bed.

"Yeah let me go and get the kids ready." He said pissed off that I haven't got back to him.

"Mommy, I don't want to go." Mya said sitting on the bed.

"Yeah me either mom." Chris said.

"Okay, you don't have to go." I said running back downstairs.

"Are you done? Where are my kids?" he said.

"They don't want to go and I am not making them." I said.

"Fine, well, I guess I'll leave." He said heading out the door. My husband came downstairs and looked at me and walked into the living room. I just don't know what the hell to do anymore.

ALICIA

I laid in bed and I heard Kia and Zakiyah yelling in their sleep. Me and Joe jumped up and headed to their room.

"Wake up baby. Wake up." We said trying to get them to wake up.

"Mommy!" they said running into my arms.

"Baby. Go ahead to bed. I got them." I said. I laid in the bed and held them in my arms. I can only imagine what my girls have been through. I am so scared because I have tired to get them to talk to me. But I know its only a moment that they need before they will talk but I know that they will.

"Lord, please guide my daughters allow them to be able to come and talk to me and for me to be able to help them. Amen."

CHAPTER 22

TIFFANY

Its been a couple of months and me and Xavier is getting closer than ever. He is very good with my children and he helps me out so much.

"Tiffany, I am going to wash up the dishes for you." He said as I went to put the kids to bed.

"I went and laid your son in the room with my boys cause he is sleeping." I said running back downstairs.

"Okay, well I done. I am going to go ahead and leave. I'll pick my son up in the morning." He said.

"No. please don't go." I said kissing him on the lips. The kiss got more powerful and it made us head upstairs to my bedroom. As he slowly laid me down and started undressing me. He had touched my body so softly and his tongue made me feel so warm inside. The way he started pounded on my ass made my body feel a way that I never felt before. Damn, it feels so damn good to be making love to a man. I cant believe that I had sex. And I do mean good sex. OH MY!

JASMINE

Damn, 2 months is along time to be living in a house of dysfunction. My husbands mad at me, my kids are upset and my house looks a mess. Damn, I cant get a break. I think my husband is trying to get back at me or something cause he has been coming home later and later from work. Sometimes I just wonder why do I even try. I cook, I clean, I feed the kids and make sure that they are ready for bed and everything. I do it all and I said sorry so many times until I am blue in the face and I am tired. I just don't even know if our marriage is going to work anymore. I sat up in the dark waiting for Deshawn to come home. But he didn't even come home at all. Wow, I just don't know what to do. I woke up and got the kids ready to go to school as my husband decides to walk into the house.

"Good morning Dad." The kids said.

"Good morning." He said kissing them on the head and headed to the stairs. Enough is enough. I cant do this.

"Deshawn, enough is enough. You have punished me enough. I said that I was sorry now what more do you want from me." I said as he turned around.

"I want you to hurt like I hurt. I want you to feel the pain of my wife having sex with another man. While my son was in here. This what I want." He said.

"Baby, I said that I was sorry. How many times can I say I am sorry Deshawn?" I said tears rolling down my face.

"Its not enough." He said running upstairs. Damn, I think that my marriage is over. I just don't know what to do. I cant keep letting my kids see me this way. I am done. I am leaving.

ALICIA

I still just don't know what to do. My daughters still dont want to talk. They bearly eat. I am so afraid. Its really about time that I talk to them. I cant see my girls like this any longer.

"Kia and Zakiyah come here please." I said.

"Honey are you sure about this." My husband said.

"Yeah." I said as they ran downstairs.

"Yes mommy." They said sitting on the couch.

"Sit down baby. I need to know what happened to you?" I said sitting between them.

"Come in babies. We are here to help you but we cant help you unless you tell us what happen." Joe said I looked into my girls faces as they broke down into tears hugging me and holding me tight. I can only imagine what he did to my daughters. I know that they wanted to talk about it but they are so scared to.

"Okay. Okay. Mommy and daddy wont make you talk. Just whenever you are ready we are here okay." I said still holding them tight. As days went by my

Daughters tried to start having just a little bit of fun. I saw them playing together. Even more they was playing with their little brother. I don't want my daughters to hold in any anger. I know that he has done a lot to them and I want to help. I gotta help by daughters. I don't like to see them down or upset. We need a change. Zakiyah's father decided to come and visit her again.

"John, what are you doing here?" I said opening the door.

"I wanted to see Zakiyah." He said.

"I don't think that's a good idea." I still standing in front of the door.

"Alicia, I want to see my daughter." He said getting upset.

"John go home. She has been through enough. Please leave." I said closing the door. I cant put my daughter through the drama. My kids has been through enough. I am not going to allow them to go through anything else. And I mean nothing else.

TIFFANY

It felt so good to wake up next to a man again. I feel like I can go a couple more rounds with him. It is just a damn good feeling to have someone touch my body so damn gently.

"Good morning Tiffany." Xavier said sitting on the edge of the bed with a hot meal.

"Wow, thank you. Are the kids up?" I said sitting up and eating.

"Yeah, they are in the kitchen eating? Do you like my surprise." He said kissing me and heading back into the kitchen with the kids. I guess that Xavier had to drop his son off at his mothers house because he left after he cleaned up my kitchen. After Xavier my sister Alicia and nieces and nephew stopped by today.

"Hey sis, What's going on your glowing?" she said sitting at the table.

"Sis, I don't know what happened I had got a feeling over me and I slept with him." I said.

"Wow, I am so happy for you Tiff. Its about time you got some." Alicia said. I could tell that my sister is going through something. She wouldn't tell me anything. Jasmine pulled up in the yard with the kids. She looked pissed to.

"Jaz, what's wrong?" I said as she sat down at the table.

"Well, a couple of months ago I slept with my ex-husband. I told Deshawn and now I think that my marriage is over." She said.

"Jaz, what happened? Sis, I am so sorry." Alicia said.

"No its my fault. I cant . . . I don't know what I am going to do. I don't know what to do. I don't know how to help her out.

"Sis, marriage is hard work. You cant only think about it being over. You got to fight for your marriage." Alicia said.

"Its so hard when he don't want to talk." She said. I don't know how it feels but I can see that my sister is hurting and I wish I knew what to say to make her feel better.

JASMINE

After talking to my sisters I know that I got to fight for my family. I love my husband and I love my kids. I cant believe that I let that happened. I cant continue to beat myself up over something that I could not change. I had sex with him. Now I want to move on.

"Deshawn, I want to move on from this pit hole that we are in right now. I love you baby and I want us to work." I said trying to figure out what to say too.

"Jaz, I want us to work on us too. I am sorry baby." He said walking up behind me.

"Baby." I said turning around and running into his arms.

"Jaz, baby I'm sorry. I am so sorry that I left you the way that I did." He said kissing me. Wow, I am glad that we want to work on us. Its about time.

CHAPTER 23

ALICIA

I love seeing a change in my girls. Kia walked into the kitchen while I made them lunch.

"Mommy, can I talk to you?" she said.

"What's wrong Kia?" I said putting chips on their plates.

"Mommy, he touched me." She said.

"He touched me you how? Did he touch you too Zakiyah?" I said stopping making the sandwich and stood in front of Kia.

"Yes mommy. He touched her too. He touched me in my private area mommy. He wouldn't stop. And when I started crying. He hit me. Mommy he continue to hit me." Kia said crying. I just grabbed my baby and held her in my arms and Zakiyah came and grabbed me too. I cant believe that he hurt my girls like this. I just don't get it. I just got to help them get up from this point. My baby girls need my help getting past this and I am going to help the get through this.

TIFFANY

I got another date with Xavier tonight. I think I might be falling in love with him. He is everything that I want a man to be. I just don't know what to expect. I am afraid to loose another man that I love. As we sat at the table Xavier kept looking into my eyes.

"What's wrong babe?" I said as he smiled.

"Tiffany, you have truly made me a happy man. Baby what I am trying to say is that I love you." He said.

"You . . . . you love me." I said with much surprise.

"Tiffany, I love you. I never loved you as much as I do. I never felt this way about any woman before. You are special to me Tiffany." He said as a tear rolled down my face. Wow, it is so amazing when you think that you cant find a good man he always appear. Man, oh man I'm in love.

JASMINE

To hear my husband say that he forgive was a step. I know that I was wrong but I had to learn from it. I got a good man. I mean a real good man and I don't want to mess up my house. My husband and my kids are my world and I don't want to mess up my family. For the first time in months me and my husband had sex. And I mean good sex. He did thing that he never did before.

"Damn, babe you did . . . ." I said speechless.

"Jasmine, what was it about him that you liked?" he asked as I laid on the bed in his arms.

"Baby please." I said.

"No babe, I want to know. I am not going to get mad." He said.

"I just missed him. I am sorry it just a feeling." I said.

"Babe, I love you and I forgave you because if I didn't our marriage couldn't work. And there is nothing that matters more to me than you and our kids." He said kissing me.

"I love you too baby and I wont hurt you again." I said as he held me in his arms. I am so happy that our marriage is back together. God has blessed me this time. I know that I cant mess up again.

ALICIA

I am glad that my baby came and told me me what happened to them and I cant stand him for what he did but he can never do it again because he was killed but now my girls need therapy again. As I resigned them up for therapy I felt good because I know that my kids will get the help that they need. I waited in the waiting room again with Jay as they talked to the therapist. I just hope that they really get all of their problems out and fixed. I really don't want them to hurt anymore. I cant see it.

"Hey mommy big boy." I said as my now 4 month old baby smiled. He is a joyful little boy. After 30 minutes later Kia and Zakiyah came out with a smiled.

"How did it go?" I asked.

"Mommy, I feel a little bit better." Kia said.

"I'm okay mommy." Zakiyah said. I am so happy at least it helped out a little. I know that its going to take more than just one visit but I hope it will help.

TIFFANY

I have started to see a new me. A new attitude of myself and everything.

"Mommy, are you okay." Nia said as I was getting dressed.

"Yeah, I am good. Go get ready to go baby." I said. Nia walked out the room shocked. I guess its because my baby never see this happy before. I love Xavier he stands and take care of my kids and he just helps with everything that I need help with. I never knew that I could fall in love the way that I have. Thank you god for sending a good man.

CHAPTER 24

JASMINE

A lot has happened to me this year. I almost lost my kids. I cheated on my husband and I am now pregnant again. Sometimes struggling means a lot man we know. I had to struggle to keep my family together. I had to learn that my husband and my kids means a lot to me. I made a mistake and I learned from it. But sometimes we struggles in ways that we don't even know. For the power to love again even when he believed that he cant. And now he have given me another seed. I give birth in 7 months but he knows that no matter what we go through God makes a way for a brighter day.

ALICIA

My year has been hell. My daughters got kidnapped and raped and Kia's father was murdered. It took a lot for me to hold it together for my girls. Struggling is so easy. Everyday I am struggling to help my girls to forgive the wrong the wrong that was done to them or even for me to put aside my feelings to show my kids that life has its up and down but you got to believe that you can make it. Its always some kind of test that you have to go through. It might be hard. Sometimes but you got to keep pushing. Keep believing that you can make it. Its inside of you all you have to do is believe in you and you can make it. I see a change in my family. My husband is blessing to me with his support. My girls are smiling more and Jay is getting bigger and older. Struggle will not hold us down. No way no how.

TIFFANY

My year might had started off wrong because I couldn't get over Antonio but I have find a man that loves me and my kids. Sometimes we struggle to get over someone we love because we are not over them. I had to start thinking about me and my kids. But the best way to end a year is by planning a wedding. Xavier and I plans to get married in the Spring. I got a new son and he got 2 more sons and 2 daughters. At first getting over Antonio was hard. I love him I still do but now I got a husband that has my love for ever and a day. Struggle is something I don't any more!